David Bell has been writing stories since he was a child.

He still writes every day.

Dawn Gray is his first comic trilogy.

Also by David Bell

Dawn Gray's Cosmic Adventure
being Part One of the Dawn Gray trilogy.

dawn gray's pyjamas in space

being Part Two of the Dawn Gray trilogy.

DAVID BELL

RANS☽M

Dawn Gray's Pyjamas in Space

by David Bell

Published by Ransom Publishing Ltd.
Rose Cottage, Howe Hill, Watlington, Oxon. OX49 5HB
www.ransom.co.uk

ISBN   184167 580 6
        978 184167 580 0

Cover design by Snowbooks

A CIP catalogue record of this book is available from the British Library.

For Joanne

my wife, my best friend and my severest critic!

prologue

beginning at the beginning

In the beginning there was the Earth, the most populated planet in the Galaxy. Home to billions upon billions of life forms, from the smallest of microscopic bacteria to the largest known mammal, the blue whale.

And then the Earth was gone, removed from the solar system like an orange plucked from a fruit bowl.

And that's that really; that was the beginning. Sixty-five million years of human evolution, billions of species, billions more forms of organic life gone in the blink of an eye: wiped out, discarded, forgotten.

So what else is there left to tell? Where is *this* story going to begin?

Well, *this* story is going to begin at the end; that is to say, it's going to begin at the beginning.

It is the end of the Earth, the end of humankind, the end of time itself.

But it is the beginning of an adventure; an adventure that, by the end, will probably have you scratching your head and wondering if the beginning really was the end or if the end was, in actual fact, just a new beginning.

So let us begin now at the end; but, don't forget … *this* is just the beginning …

1

earth (friday 12:28am)

As the giant spaceship hung in the night sky, eclipsing the Sun and casting a dark, ominous shadow over the world below it, a single, lone figure watched, perfectly calmly, with the most bemused expression on her face.

Her name was Fizz and she had been here before.

She was standing on the front lawn of number twenty-eight Kirkland Street, watching as people panicked all around her, screaming and pointing in horror at the strange, screwdriver-shaped spaceship hovering high above them.

Fizz blinked slowly as she watched the residents of Kirkland Street dash about like so many headless chickens, all of them terrified: wondering what the ship was, where it had come from and what was going to happen next.

Fizz knew what was going to happen next.

As I said … she'd been here before and she was dressed and ready for it.

She had sunglasses on for a start and, considering that it was the middle of the night, wearing sunglasses was a sure sign that she knew *something*. On her head was a swimming cap, covered in Vaseline; around her neck was a pair of fluffy earmuffs; and she was covered in light-green sunblock and was chewing gum.

The spaceship climbed higher into the night sky, pointing upwards silently. Fizz didn't move; she didn't even seem particularly bothered that the ship was there.

Everyone around her continued to scream and then a man and a woman, dressed in the same bizarre way that Fizz was, beckoned to her from the middle of the front lawn.

"Fizz!" the man called out. He looked middle-aged and he looked petrified. "Fizz! Come on!"

Fizz noticed the couple sitting cross-legged on the lawn. There was something that looked a little bit like a firework sticking up from the ground between them.

"Fizz?" the woman sitting next to the man said. "What are you doing?"

"Mr Gray?" Fizz whispered to herself. "Mrs Gray?"

She walked across the lawn to where the couple sat and stared at them for a moment, completely baffled.

"Fizz, don't we have to go?" Mr Gray pleaded. "You said you could help us. You said you could save us somehow. Do you remember that, Fizz?"

"It's no good, Geoffrey," Mrs Gray said, pulling her earmuffs on and straightening her sunglasses. "The poor girl has completely lost her marbles." Mrs Gray pointed at the strange-looking stick in the ground. It had a label hanging off it. Written on this label were the words:

YOU CAN PULL NOW!

"Fizz!" Mr Gray shouted, jumping to his feet and taking Fizz firmly by the shoulders. "Fizz! Listen to me! You told us earlier this evening that this ..." – Mr Gray gestured to the gigantic spaceship hanging above them in the sky – "this ... Trygo ... Traygan ..."

"Trygonian Council Recovery Vessel," Fizz finished.

"Right, Trygonian thingamajig, was coming to tow the Earth away and kill everyone on it. Do you remember that?"

She wasn't really sure how or why, but Fizz was certain that she did remember that. She remembered that she was a Galaxy Guide, working for The Galactic Association for Galaxy Guides and LX Travellers. She remembered that she had been sent to Earth to save someone, to evacuate someone before the Earth was towed away and sentenced to be doomed. But she couldn't remember who it was.

Fizz just nodded.

"Right," Mr Gray went on. "And you told us that you could evacuate us, get us off Earth before that happened. You said this thing ..." – Mr Gray pointed to the stick in the ground – "was an ... LX ..."

"Dome," Fizz finished again.

"An LX Dome, right, and that it could zap us to safety in a split-second and save us all."

Fizz just nodded again, but she didn't say another word.

Mr Gray waited.

Mrs Gray waited.

Nobody said anything.

"Are you going to save us?!" Mr Gray eventually bellowed. "Fizz! It's started! The Trygonians are here! Are you going to save us?!"

It's strange how, all of a sudden, something just comes to you. Without any prompting a thought, a realisation, suddenly flashes into your head, something so obvious that the fact that you didn't realise it before is almost ridiculous.

"Oh, my GOD!" Fizz suddenly screamed. Her outburst was so ferocious that Mr Gray actually stumbled back and fell sprawling over his wife's feet. "Where's Dawn?!"

Mr Gray sat himself up and stared at his wife.

Mrs Gray stared right back at her husband, their faces vacant and blank.

"Who's Dawn?" Mr Gray said to Fizz.

"Dawn who?" Mrs Gray added.

Fizz opened her mouth to explain but, for some strange reason, no words came out. She was so stunned and confused, shocked and utterly bemused that the Grays didn't know who she was talking about, that she simply couldn't find the words.

"Dawn," she finally managed to mumble. "Dawn Gray. Your daughter."

Mr and Mrs Gray looked at each other again.

"Um, Fizz," Mr Gray said. "We don't have a daughter."

When things suddenly stop for no apparent reason – and by *things* I mean people, spaceships, time itself – it takes the brain a few seconds to realise what has happened. There is, of course, no way for me to prove this to you here and now, so you'll just have to take my word for it when I tell you that when the Grays suddenly froze, Fizz didn't really notice. She continued to rant and rave about Dawn Gray, about how she was Mr and Mrs Gray's daughter, and about how she should be here right now and how something was terribly, *terribly* wrong.

It was only when Fizz took a moment to look around her and noticed that every other resident of Kirkland Street was frozen, that she realised time had come to a complete stop.

People were just perfectly still, like waxworks. Some were in mid-run; some were huddled on the floor trying to scream; some were even in the middle of hugging a loved one. No matter what the people of Kirkland Street had been in the middle of doing just a few moments ago, they were now all frozen in time.

Even the ship hanging in the sky above the Earth was frozen. The lights at the back had stopped flashing and its ascent had stopped. It was just hanging there, like a gigantic cardboard cut-out that had been stuck on the front of the Moon.

Suddenly, the Earth beneath Fizz's feet began to tremble. She lifted her sunglasses onto the top of her head and peered around in the gloomy night to try and locate the source of the unnerving rumbling sound that seemed to be coming her way.

And then she saw it. A short way away from her a solid, metallic ball was hurtling towards her at great speed. Fizz thought about running, but soon realised that the ball was going too fast. Anyway, there was nowhere to run to

2

queeg

By the time the ball had reached Fizz and come to a stop, she had already decided that she was in trouble. Fizz had been travelling the Galaxy long enough to know that strange and bizarre things turning up and stopping time, whether they are humanoid in form or just big, heavy-looking metal balls, wasn't something that happened unless something somewhere was seriously wrong. And, when things had gone seriously wrong, Fizz could always safely bet that it was something to do with her.

At first the ball, which was about twice the size of a beach ball, just rocked back and forth on the ground. Fizz considered touching it or trying to see if there was anything inside it; but then she realised that she wasn't really *that* stupid, and so she decided to try and stand as far back from it as she could, while trying not to *look* as though she was standing as far back from it as she could on purpose.

And then, quite unexpectedly, the ball began clicking and beeping. Fizz took another step back, still trying not to look as if she was keeping her distance, as four little doors flipped open, two on either side of the metal ball. Two long, wiry, little legs suddenly shot out from two of the doors, and two equally spindly arms appeared from the other two. In comparison to the size and apparent weight of the ball itself, these legs and arms were ridiculously thin and long: they resembled wire coat hangers that had been bent straight and had had little metal feet and hands stuck on the ends.

The legs, fully extended, began hoisting the metal ball up until it was balancing somewhat unsteadily.

Another little door suddenly zipped open, this one on the very top of the ball, and from inside it appeared what could best be described as an upside-down lampshade with eyes.

These glowing yellow eyes blinked hard a couple of times and then focused on Fizz. The lampshade, which Fizz now assumed was this strange creature's head, rose up a little higher from inside its round metal body to reveal a mouth: a mouth that was grinning inanely.

"Greetings," the creature said in a rasping, metallic voice, before proceeding to cough and splutter for a good ten seconds. "Excuse me, space travel doesn't agree with me any more. At my age, space dust gets into the old circuitry and gives me circuitritis, you know?"

Fizz nodded.

"'Course," she said. "Circuitritis. That can be nasty."

"Allow me to introduce myself," the creature went on, still trying to clear his throat. "I am Queeg, Superintendent and Regulator for the Space-Time Vortex."

Fizz sighed heavily. She had thought for some horrible second that she was in trouble, but now she knew that she was in big, *big* trouble.

3

the time tunnel

Isn't it amazing how, all of a sudden, without being able to help it, you can just *look* GUILTY.

Fizz did, the moment she found out who Queeg was.

Queeg was known throughout the Galaxy, though few beings had ever actually come across him. The Space-Time Vortex, the very foundation that the Galaxy itself was built on, was an intricate, baffling series of pockets of time and dimensions. Every living being, every planet, every solar system existed within the Vortex, as did every alternative reality. Queeg was the caretaker, for want of a better word, who made sure that everything was in order and in check. It was Queeg who ensured that no two dimensions ever clashed and that no two times ever crossed paths. For Queeg himself to come and see Fizz personally meant, automatically, that she had done something seriously wrong.

Fizz had a suspicion of what she had done that was so wrong to demand Queeg's presence, and at once she began defending herself.

"Listen, okay?" she began, holding her hands up in a gesture of surrender. "I know what you're going to say. I know why you're here and I admit it … I messed up, all right? But I can fix it, honestly; I can sort it out – just … just give me a bit of time."

"Do not fear, Galaxy Guide," Queeg said, kindly, still coughing and spluttering. "You do not have to explain yourself to me. I have not come here to arrest you."

Fizz felt a sudden swell of relief rush through her, but it was quickly followed by a second swell of something else: not relief, but anxiety.

"Well … why are you here, then?" she asked nervously.

"I am here," Queeg said, "to ask you to take on a special assignment, a job. A mission, if you like."

Fizz thought a moment about what to say next. She didn't like the sound of the words "special assignment" and "mission".

"Do I have to take this … *mission*?" she asked.

"No! Of course not!" Queeg replied, chuckling to himself. Fizz breathed another sigh of relief.

"Oh, that's okay then."

"Not if you *want* to be the cause of the entire Galaxy imploding and every living organism in existence becoming extinct in the blink of an eye."

Fizz's heart sank.

"However," Queeg went on, happily, "if you were interested in becoming the saviour of the Galaxy and the saviour of every living organism in existence, then you may want to hear more. Which do you choose: saviour or exterminator?"

There was something about Queeg that Fizz was beginning, incredibly quickly, to dislike. He seemed a happy but bumbling sort of creature, the kind of being who would never have a bad word to say about anyone or anything. But the more he went on, the more Fizz thought that he hadn't come to her to *ask* if she would take on a 'special assignment' but to *tell* her to take it on – or else. Beneath the exterior of his cheerfully round body, his spindly arms and legs and his ridiculously-shaped head, Fizz guessed he was a creature who was the Superintendent of the Space–Time Vortex for a reason. Queeg was not a being to mess with.

"Okay," she said gloomily. "What do I have to do?"

Before Queeg could answer, the most peculiar sound pierced the air. It sounded a little bit like a pop, only it was more of a *Zop*!

At first, Fizz didn't pay the sound any attention. It was only when a swirl of thick black smoke began to pour out of the control panel on the front of Queeg's round body that she realised ... he'd been shot.

Zop!

The sound went again, louder this time. Queeg stumbled forward on his thin legs, lost his footing and toppled past Fizz, crashing onto the front lawn of number twenty-eight Kirkland Street.

Zop!

The sound went again. Queeg himself was wobbling on the ground, smoke pouring up from his body, his thin arms and legs flopping uselessly beside him. Fizz knelt on the grass beside him and looked into his green eyes, which were fading like a candle slowly burning out.

"You ... must ... go," Queeg hissed, his rasping, metallic voice crackling and breaking up as he spoke. "They are looking for her ... as I was ... and now ... as you must."

"Dawn?" Fizz said instinctively.

Slowly, Queeg reached out one of his thin, spindly arms and laid it on the ground next to him.

In his hand, Fizz could see what looked like a solid, silver toilet-roll tube. It had a tiny little monitor on one end and, on this monitor, a series of numbers were flashing.

"What's that?" she asked, nervously.

"It is called … a Time Tunnel," Queeg replied. "It can transport you great distances in an instant. You could leave Earth now and arrive on Pluto in a matter of seconds."

Fizz studied the little silver tube.

"It looks a bit … small for me, don't you think?"

Queeg said nothing. Instead, he simply tapped the silver tube on the ground. There was a flash of light and in an instant the tube had expanded to five times its size and had grown to such a length that Fizz could no longer see the end of it. It looked like a giant aqua-slide running across the entire length of Kirkland Street and beyond.

"That's cool," Fizz said, calmly.

"Get in," Queeg coughed.

"What?"

"No time … to explain. Soon … they will be here. Get … in."

A strong whooshing sound started to come from the open end of the giant silver tunnel; air was being sucked into it like a vacuum cleaner.

"You know, I think I'm gonna pass, if it's all the same with you," Fizz said, politely. "I mean, clearly you want me to go somewhere but, if you just give me the coordinates,

I've got an LX Dome that'll take me anywhere I wanna go. So ..."

"SILENCE!" Queeg bellowed with what little breath he had left. "The LX Dome cannot take you where you need to go." Again, Queeg rolled his large, spherical frame back and forth as pain seemed to surge through him. "In just a moment ... I will be dead, and if you do not go now ... you will be too. There is no time left for me to explain. Just ... get in."

Fizz looked at Queeg. She looked at the giant Time Tunnel, laid out for miles ahead of her. It was now sucking air into it with ferocious power.

"Oh, I do not believe this," Fizz grumbled. She removed her swimming hat, sunglasses and earmuffs and stuffed them into the black hip bag that was secured around her waist. She scrambled on her hands and knees towards the open end of the tunnel.

"This has been just like the worst week of my life. I don't know *how* I get myself into these things, I really don't. I mean, who cares about me, huh? Who wonders how *I m* doing? It's all the Galaxy this, Dawn that. I am *so* sick of it, I really think I need a holiday."

Fizz laid her legs just inside the entrance of the Time Tunnel and immediately felt herself being sucked into it. She held tightly onto the rim of the tunnel as she looked back at Queeg.

"We will meet again soon, Galaxy Guide," Queeg gasped. "May time be on your side. Now ... go ... they are here."

The last thing Fizz saw was an army of enormous, gruesome-looking shadows towering over Queeg.

There was a flurry of bright laser fire, then Queeg disappeared amidst a thick cloud of smoke and flames.

Fizz let go of the rim of the Tunnel and was instantly sucked inside.

Everything went black.

4

dawn's strange encounter

Dawn Gray was a reasonably well-adjusted, thirteen year-old girl. She was level-headed, mild-mannered and extremely understanding.

At least, she thought she was.

Recent events in Dawn's life, however, had begun to bring about a change in her: a change in her mood, in her outlook on life and in her very temperament.

As she trudged along the dry, dusty ground of the nameless planet she now found herself on, Dawn Gray was beginning to feel … angry, irritable … bad tempered.

And well she might. After all – wouldn't you? Dawn Gray had, in a relatively short space of time, gone from being a perfectly average thirteen-year-old girl, delivering the local paper for some pocket money, to being some sort of galactic outcast. She was lost in the furthest reaches of space, dressed in her fluffy white slippers and pink pyjamas and armed only with a pair of sunglasses, a pair of earmuffs and some chewing gum, all of which were stuffed into a black hip bag that was fastened around her waist.

Add to that the fact that Dawn had now experienced the end of the Earth and of mankind itself – twice; the fact that she had no idea where her parents were; and that the only people on the planet she was on were hundreds, possibly even thousands, of alternative Dawn Grays – and you will, I'm sure, begin to sympathise with Dawn and her slightly less-than-cheerful mood.

It was true that, shortly after arriving on this planet, Dawn had had an ingenious idea that she believed would help her escape from it, this planet where there were only thousands of other Dawn Grays for company. But now, as she walked miserably along, beneath two scorching suns, she was beginning to think that her brilliant idea had been nothing more than a vague hope and one that could not possibly work.

Dawn stopped somewhere roughly between the last big rock she had passed and the next big rock, which was a little way ahead of her, and looked around.

There was nothing here. The ground was dusty and red, burnt to a cinder beneath the suns. There were no plants, no trees, no water, nothing at all. There was certainly no sign of what she was desperately looking for.

The only thing Dawn could see was …

… a funny-looking girl in funny woolly clothes.

Dawn rubbed her eyes and blinked hard, as the odd looking girl walked towards her. The girl seemed to have appeared from nowhere; there was simply nowhere for her to have appeared from. But there she was, clear as day, walking awkwardly towards Dawn with a gormless smile on her face as she waved manically.

"Hello," the girl said cheerily, as she finally reached Dawn.

"All right?" Dawn replied hesitantly.

"Dawn Gray, right?" the girl said, waving a finger at Dawn.

"Uh … yeah, one of many on this planet."

The girl suddenly broke into the most atrocious, snorting laugh; she sounded like a pig with asthma having some kind of seizure.

Dawn took a cautious step back.

"That's a good one!" the girl roared. "One of many! Of course, there are only Dawn Grays on this planet, aren't there?! That's a good one!" The girl began her snorting roar of laughter again, and Dawn took another step back.

The girl's clothes were full of holes. They looked a little like pyjamas, but they were filthy, tatty and frayed all around the seams, and the girl herself looked grubby, to put it politely.

"You've met the others, then?" the girl said, when she finally stopped laughing and caught her breath.

"Yeah," Dawn replied, carefully. She didn't want to say anything funny; she didn't want to set the weird little girl off laughing again. "Only for a minute, seeing hundreds of me was a bit disturbing, you know?"

"Tell me about it," the girl replied, pushing back a greasy, matted fringe of dark hair away from her face. "When I first saw them, I nearly peed myself! Course, they didn't really want me around, so I didn't stay too long." The girl's face changed and Dawn thought she noticed a little sadness in her eyes. "I was one too many, I think," she said. "Mind you, I suppose you would have been welcome; you're the prettiest of us all."

Dawn stared at the girl. They were quite different. Dawn was a lot taller than her. She was certainly cleaner than her. Their hair was a different colour and their dress sense was worlds apart – but, for some strange reason, there was something familiar about her.

"You were one too many?" Dawn said, softly. "Why? What's your name?"

The funny-looking girl smiled and held out her hand to Dawn.

"Dawn Gray," she said happily. "Pleased to meet you."

5

squig

She really thought she was going to die.

Travelling by Time Tunnel was a new and revolutionary mode of transport, even in Galactic terms; Fizz had never tried it before and she intended, if she survived this experience, never to try it again.

Imagine, if you can, being wrapped up tightly in cling film and stuffed inside a big, tall refrigerator while someone tugged and pulled on your ankles as hard as they could. If you can imagine that, you can imagine just a little bit of the discomfort of travelling by Time Tunnel.

Unfortunately for Fizz, on top of the incredibly uncomfortable and terrifying experience she was going through, she had absolutely no idea – having never travelled by Time Tunnel before – that an individual travelling by this method has no ability to move their facial muscles whilst zipping through the tunnel. They are quite simply going too fast, and the pressure of being sucked through the tunnel is so great that every muscle in your body freezes.

Upon entering the Time Tunnel, Fizz exclaimed a single phrase of shock and panic. That phrase was: "*Oh, poo!*"

And now, as she zoomed through the tunnel, all that could be heard at either end was a bellowed, echoing:

"POOOOOOOOOOOOOOOOOOOOOOOOOOOOOOO OOOOOO!"

If she was to die during this experience, Fizz thought, as she hurtled through the darkness, the Galaxy would know that she was the first person to die travelling by Time Tunnel who screamed the immortal, famous last word: "Poo." If she could have cringed at the thought at that moment, then she would have done so.

It would be fair to say that, when she stopped flying through the Time Tunnel, Fizz was a little shocked, especially considering that she didn't seem to have arrived anywhere. She had just stopped in the middle of the tunnel, her exclamation of "*Poo!*" still echoing all around the darkness, her muscles still paralysed, her face still frozen.

Suddenly, just inches above where she was lying, face up, trapped in the narrow tube of the Time Tunnel, a hatch opened and a horrible-looking red thing appeared. It looked a little bit like a new-born puppy, without the fur and covered in strawberry jelly. It was completely hairless, completely toothless and looked horribly squished and cramped in its little compartment above the Time Tunnel. The only thing it had on was a big, thick pair of goggles, behind which two huge, magnified eyes were squinting down at Fizz, who still could not move or speak very well.

"Evening to you," the little red thing croaked, in a whiny sort of squeak. "My name is Squig; I'm your Travel Inspector for this journey in the Time Tunnel. Destination please?"

"What?" Fizz managed to mumble through her frozen mouth.

"Destination?" Squig repeated. "You've just travelled through a very important STV Zone."

Fizz looked blank.

"A Space-Time Vortex Zone," Squig explained.

Fizz just glared at the creature above her, who was only an inch or so from her face. She forced her lips to move as well as they could.

"Ah ya joiking ma?"

The squished little creature's huge eyes blinked inquisitively.

"What did you say?" he croaked.

Fizz tried to speak again, but her jaw ached now and she was beginning to dribble.

"Destination … please!" Squig repeated again, a real hint of irritation creeping into his voice now.

"Ah dan't nah!" Fizz screamed.

"What?" Squig bellowed back.

"Ah dan't nah!" Fizz screamed again.

"I can't understand a word you're saying!" Squig's eyes were beginning to turn red with anger.

"AH – DAN'T – NAH!" Fizz screamed as best she could. Her jaw was throbbing now and she was drooling like a hungry dog, but her arms were trapped by her sides in the narrow tunnel so she couldn't wipe her chin or rub her jaw. "AH – DAN'T – KNAH!" she screamed again. "AH – DAN'T – KNAH! AH – DAN'T – KNAH! I – DON'T – KNOW!"

Finally, some feeling returned to Fizz's jaw and she sighed with relief.

"You don't know?" Squig repeated. "What do you mean, you don't know?"

"I don't know where I'm going," Fizz muttered, wincing as her jaw continued to ache. "I didn't know I needed to have a destination; I didn't buy a ticket, you know! This isn't a flippin' bus!"

Slowly, Squig poked his hairless, toothless, slimy head out of the hatchway so he was nose to nose with Fizz.

"It's down the chute with you, then," he hissed.

"The chute?" Fizz repeated nervously. "Is … *that* like being on a bus?"

The creature giggled and pulled himself back into his hatch.

"Not really," he said. "Not that I have even the faintest idea what a bus is, but it's more like falling through space and having your brain sucked out through your nose."

Fizz gulped.

"Wait!" she screamed. "I *am* going somewhere! I don't know where exactly, but I am going *somewhere!*"

"Sorry," Squig said, not sounding as if he was sorry at all. "No destination, no riding the Time Tunnel: that's the rule."

"But I am, HONESTLY!" Fizz exclaimed, wriggling as best she could in the vain hope that she could escape the drastic situation she now found herself in.

"Rule 7633.1 of the Time Tunnel Travellers' Rule Book and Guide states, quite clearly, that any being found riding the Time Tunnel without a specific destination or a valid pass or permit must be ejected via the chute." Squig glared at Fizz, his wide eyes narrowing menacingly behind his huge goggles. "No exceptions."

"Queeg sent me!" Fizz bellowed, suddenly remembering the name. "Queeg! You know him? The Superintendent and Regulator for the Space-Time Vortex!"

Squig stared at Fizz a moment.

"Yes, yes! The Superintendent, that's him!" Fizz agreed.

"And where exactly was he sending you?" Squig asked, suspiciously.

"I have absolutely no idea," Fizz said, completely honestly. "I wouldn't bother phoning him to ask though – I don't think he's gonna be up for a chat right now, you know?"

Squig glared at Fizz again and poked his horrible red head out of the hatch again.

"I don't like you," he hissed. "I don't like you one bit."

"Well, I have to tell you," Fizz replied calmly, "that I'm not gonna lose sleep over that."

"Branch Tunnel A!" Squig spat angrily, as he twisted round behind him and pulled a lever. "Elbows in: it's gonna be bumpy!" Squig began to laugh manically as Fizz suddenly felt herself being sucked down again.

"Wait a minute!" she screamed. "What's down Branch Tunnel A?"

There wasn't time for her to hear an answer.

The Time Tunnel pulled her down into darkness again.

As she disappeared downwards, Fizz could hear Squig laughing behind her.

In just a few minutes her journey would be over, but the bad day she was already having would start to get a whole lot worse.

6

the other dawn gray

"I don't understand," Dawn said, sitting down on a rock. "You're Dawn Gray? Like … an alternative *me*?"

The funny-looking girl sat down on the rock next to Dawn and a cloud of smelly dust puffed up from her clothes.

"Yep," she replied, smiling. "Shocked?"

"Not shocked," Dawn replied. "Surprised. Confused a bit. I saw the other Dawn Grays when I arrived here, all the other alternative versions of me – all the other Dawn Grays from different times, different dimensions. They all looked … well, they all looked like me."

"But I don't, do I?" the girl said.

"No," Dawn replied. "You don't at all."

"I'm the runt of the litter," the girl said, her smile fading slightly, the hint of sadness creeping back into her eyes. "Apparently, every being has one."

"I don't get it," Dawn said.

"Well, you know all about alternative dimensions and stuff, right?" the girl said. She was picking at one of the moth-eaten holes in her woolly pyjama top. "Fizz told you all about that, yeah?"

"You know Fizz?" Dawn said.

"'Course. Most of my life has been the same as yours, the same as all those other Dawn Grays you met. We've all lived the same lives, just in different times, different dimensions. A few things have been different; we've each chosen different paths, gone different ways here and there, but we were all evacuated from the Earth when it was towed. We all knew Fizz and Fizz, being the idiot she is, got the evacuation wrong and landed us all here over and over again. You'd think she'd have learned her mistake after making it a few hundred times, wouldn't you?"

Dawn shook her head, trying to clear her mind and get her thoughts together. She was starting to feel a bit lost again; Galactic time travel and dimension-hopping took some understanding.

"So ..." – Dawn hesitated, trying to choose her words carefully; she did not want to offend her funny-looking namesake – "... so why do you look so different from me, then? If you're just a different me ... from a different time?"

"Because, like I said, I'm the runt of the litter," the girl replied. "Every being has alternative versions of themselves throughout the Galaxy, across the Space-Time Vortex. Different dimension, different pocket of time: different Dawn Gray. You're all pretty much the same – lived the same life, made the same choices, met the same people."

"Like Fizz," Dawn interrupted.

"Exactly," the girl agreed. "But while every being in the Galaxy has hundreds or thousands of alternative versions of themselves, they also have two completely opposite versions: one that made all the right choices, got all the luck, did everything right; and one who did everything wrong and got none of the luck."

Dawn stared at the girl in amazement and suddenly realised who she was looking at. This funny-looking girl in the worn, torn clothes was her. This girl was the Dawn Gray living somewhere in time who was destined to fail at everything she tried; this girl was the Dawn Gray who was never going to be lucky.

Dawn suddenly saw herself in the girl, suddenly saw her own face beneath the lank hair and greasy, grubby skin, and she felt as if she wanted to cry.

"You're me," she whispered, as the realisation swept over her.

The girl nodded.

"Yep. I'm the you who has suffered every day of her life. I'm the Dawn Gray whose parents died when she was just six months old. I'm the Dawn Gray who's grown up in so many different orphanages and foster homes that I can't even remember them all. I'm the Dawn Gray who can't read or write. I'm the Dawn Gray who has no friends, no money, no home and no family."

Dawn felt her heart skip a beat; she had to bite down on her lip to stop tears escaping. She felt so sorry for this girl, this alternative Dawn Gray, that she didn't know how to begin apologising.

"I don't know what to say," Dawn said, softly, reaching out and holding the girl's hand. "I feel … I feel so guilty."

The funny-looking girl looked up at Dawn. Tears were running down her cheeks; they smeared the dirt on her face, making clean streaks all the way down to her chin.

"It shouldn't be like this," Dawn went on. "I've had everything. I live in a nice house, both my parents are alive – at least, I *think* they're still alive. I've got nothing to complain about."

"Don't worry," the girl said. "Somewhere out there is another Dawn Gray who's a lot better off than you. A Dawn Gray who was born into a wealthy family, who lives in a mansion in Hollywood or something; a Dawn Gray who is better looking, cleverer and more popular than you."

Dawn felt a jolt in her heart. She didn't like to admit it to herself but, she guessed, she was feeling … envy.

"It's just the way it is. That Dawn Gray is rich and lives in her world, in her time. You and I live in our own worlds and our own times. Don't feel bad for me; there's nothing we can do about it."

Just then, a flicker of blue light on the horizon caught Dawn's eye and her heart leapt. She knew exactly what it was.

"Oh yes, there is," she said, jumping to her feet excitedly. "There is something I can do about it."

The other Dawn Gray watched Dawn in total bemusement.

"What … er … what ya doing?"

"I had an idea when I got here," Dawn said, as she stared across the barren land in front of her, watching as the eerie, electric-blue light flickered on and off and on again. "I don't know why it suddenly came to me; it's something that happened to me not long ago that gave me the idea." She turned and looked at the girl. "And it is a brilliant idea. A bit dodgy, probably a bit dangerous, but I think it'll work and it's worth the risk. It beats spending the rest of our lives stuck on this dump with only thousands of different versions of us for company, right?"

The girl looked completely lost.

"If you say so," she said. "What do you mean though, 'it beats spending the rest of *our* lives stuck here'?"

Dawn smiled and knelt down in front of the funny-looking girl called Dawn Gray.

"I think I know how to get off this planet and start again, and I want you to come with me," she said. "Call it a favour; call it a payback for me being the lucky Dawn Gray and you being the one who had the cruddy life. Call it whatever you like. All I know is I've met you now. You may be me, I may be you; but I think you've suffered enough and I want to help you start again and make a better life. You up for it?"

The girl smiled.

"'Course I am!" she exclaimed. "But how are we going to get off this planet?"

"Follow me," Dawn said, pulling the other Dawn up on to her feet. "I'll show you."

1

the eye of the galaxy

There are many unexplained phenomena in the Galaxy. Take the Rygona Blimpleberger, for instance: the biggest three-legged, seven-headed, luminous-yellow mammal in the entire universe. True, the Rygona Blimpleberger is the *only* three-legged, seven-headed, luminous-yellow mammal in the entire universe, but, nevertheless, the creature is the biggest of its kind and a phenomenon.

And what about the Tik Tak? No, not the tasty little minty sweet you can eat by the handful that *we* all know; the Galactic Tik Tak is in fact the smallest being alive anywhere in the Galaxy, on *any* planet. Seven hundred and thirty-three millionths of a millimetre in length, the Tik Tak is invisible to any eye, even if it were studied under the most powerful microscope; and yet, this teeny, tiny little creature eats the same amount of food in one day that the entire population of Belgium eats in a month – but it never grows any bigger.

However, perhaps the greatest, most mysterious phenomenon of them all is The Eye of the Galaxy, inside the Vaga Portal.

The Vaga Portal is, as the name suggests, a doorway, an entrance, a threshold one passes through to enter into what is most commonly known as The Eye of the Galaxy.

It's like the eye of a hurricane or tornado. It is the exact centre of the Galaxy and, from within the Eye, anyone can see anything, at any time, in any dimension, anywhere.

The Vaga Portal is not guarded. It is not protected, as you would think it would be, by fleets of ships and soldiers; it doesn't need to be. There are no coordinates for The Vaga Portal; there are no directions. Nobody knows it exists, nobody knows it is there. Therefore, nobody has ever tried to find it and, quite simply, nobody has ever even come close to discovering it.

Until now …

The first thing Fizz noticed was a swirling of cloudy colour all around her. She had stopped hurtling down the Time Tunnel and now, much to her surprise and, she had to admit, great relief, she found herself sitting upright on what appeared to be … a big, red … squirrel.

For the briefest of moments Fizz considered addressing the squirrel, perhaps to ask exactly where she was or how she got there. But after noticing that the animal was nibbling away quite happily on a preposterously oversized nut, and considering that the squirrel had teeth the size of bath mats, she thought that for the time being she would just keep her mouth shut, try and get a grip on herself and see what happened next.

The swirling mass of coloured cloud all around her was quite unlike anything she had ever seen. Every colour imaginable was mixed into it, but the cloud itself seemed to change shape and form, almost as though it were being ordered to do so.

There were voices too, coming from inside the cloud: languages Fizz recognised, and some she didn't. There really were too many voices for her to pick any one out, but she could be sure that there were male and female, young and old voices, all seeming to come from far behind the shape-shifting cloud.

The squirrel didn't seem to mind his newly acquired passenger. Quite the contrary, in fact, because when he had finished eating the enormous nut he turned around and looked Fizz straight in the eye before saying:

"All right?"

Fizz went to speak, but the only sound that came out of her mouth was a kind of gabble that went "Whowhenwhatwhyhowhmmmm?" She wasn't really sure what she had meant to say but, amazingly, the squirrel did.

"I am Hobey," he said, in his disturbingly human-sounding voice. "You just arrived here from the Time Tunnel. This is The Eye of the Galaxy; you're here to receive a very important mission. And how do I know? Well, because Queeg sent you."

"Thanks," Fizz said.

"No problemo," Hobey replied. "Shall we go?"

"Go?" Fizz repeated. "Go where?"

"Queeg and Sarkon are waiting to see you. Ready?"

"Queeg?" Fizz suddenly felt a churn of guilt and anguish in her stomach as she realised she was about to be the bearer of bad news. "Sorry but … I think Queeg is … dead."

Hobey began roaring with laughter and, it has to be said, if you put yourself in Fizz's shoes for a moment, there is nothing more disturbing than being lost somewhere in the furthest reaches of space and sitting on the back of a giant squirrel while it screams with hysterical, near-maniacal laughter.

"Queeg … dead?" Hobey chuckled. "Oh, that's a good one! That's a really good one!"

"Did I say something funny?" Fizz asked. She was beginning to get a little irritated over being kept in the dark about what exactly was going on here, and she didn't like it. However, she was still keen not to anger the giant squirrel; she didn't know him well enough to be sure he wouldn't nibble her head off as though she were just another big nut, should he feel suddenly inclined.

"Funny?" Hobey said. "Oh, funny, yeah, yeah, yeah, funny. You said something funny all right. Come on, I'd better show you. Oh boy, are you in for a shock. Are you in for a shock!"

Hobey began scurrying away with Fizz on his back, into the swirling, colourful cloud and towards whatever lay beyond.

8

dimension-hopping for beginners

The Space-Time Vortex was a magnificent sight to behold. Dawn had only ever seen it once before and she had learned then that it was unpredictable and highly unstable. But she had also learned that it could transport you from one point in time to another in the blink of an eye; the only problem was, you could never really be sure exactly *where* it was going to transport you to.

"What is it?" the funny-looking Dawn Gray asked, staring out across at the strange blue grid that was glowing on the horizon in front of her.

"That … is the Space–Time Vortex," Dawn replied.

"Oh," the other Dawn Gray said blankly. "What's that?"

Clearly, Dawn realised, she was not explaining herself well enough for her alternative self to understand.

"The Vortex is the blueprint for the Galaxy," Dawn answered. She wasn't entirely sure if everything she was saying was right or not; her explanation was based on what little she had learned and what she assumed and guessed at. "The entire Galaxy sits on the Vortex, right?"

The girl nodded.

The Vortex in front of her looked like a giant chessboard: an enormous grid of electric-blue light flickering and crackling on and off, parts of it slightly hidden beneath the planet's dusty ground.

"Every pocket of time, for every being, on every planet, in every dimension, sits on the Vortex, right?"

"Uh huh," the girl mumbled.

"We" Dawn went on, "are currently standing inside one square of the Vortex."

Both Dawn Grays looked down. It was true; beneath them, shining beneath the ground, was flickering blue light.

"In every other square on the grid … on the Vortex, is a different pocket of time, a different reality, a different dimension. Got it?"

"If you say so."

"I do," Dawn said abruptly. "We can't cross into a different time, into a different square on the Vortex, any more than we can walk through walls. But, if we stand here long enough, hopefully the Vortex will zap us into another dimension."

The other Dawn Gray looked worried.

"*Zap* us?" she repeated nervously. "I'm not really sure I like the sound of that."

"Oh, don't worry," Dawn replied, reassuringly. "It doesn't hurt. Look, the thing is, you can't normally *see* the Vortex. It's just – when time gets mixed up and dimensions clash and things go wrong and … well, let's face it, this planet is mixed up big-time. Thousands of us living on one planet? That qualifies as a problem with space and time, don't you think? When that happens, the Vortex kind of … malfunctions and it can be seen, like we can see it now. What it'll start to do is try to figure out where exactly we should be in the Galaxy, where exactly we should be in time, and it'll keep trying to relocate us to the right place."

"And that's how we'll get off this rock," the girl finished.

"Exactly," Dawn said, smiling, thoroughly pleased with herself and her explanation of something that she herself didn't even understand. "It's called dimension-hopping ... I think."

"But ... where will it ... *zap* us to?" the girl asked.

Dawn smiled.

"I have absolutely no idea," she replied, honestly. "All I know is, it won't be here. But we have to think quickly. When the Vortex sticks us somewhere else, it'll only take a second for it to realise that we shouldn't be there either and it'll zap us straight back here. It'll keep doing that until it finds exactly where we should be. And, considering that neither of us knows where we should be either, and we certainly shouldn't be existing anywhere *together*, that could take a long, long time."

"So what do we do?"

"When the Vortex sends us somewhere, think quickly; if you think it's safe for us to stay there, shout "Go!" We'll hold hands and just jump and grab hold of something there. So then, when the Vortex zaps the pocket of time we were in back here, we won't be in it and, hopefully, we should stay in the dimension or the reality we landed in."

There followed an eerie, slightly nervous silence.

"Hopefully?" the other Dawn Gray said. "*Hopefully* we should stay in the dimension we land in? You don't know for certain that this will work, do you?"

"Nope," Dawn replied, smiling. "But I've done it before. I haven't quite tried to control it like this, but I've seen what the Vortex can do, so I'm guessing my theory will work."

"And this is all your idea, is it?" the girl asked. "This was the idea you had when you got here not long ago. This was your brilliant idea, was it?"

Dawn just nodded.

"Yep. This is it."

The two Dawn Grays smiled at each other.

"It is brilliant," the funny-looking girl said.

"Thank you," Dawn replied.

"It's completely bonkers," the girl went on. "Insanity, suicide, utter and total suicidal madness. But it is brilliant."

All of a sudden, the Space-Time Vortex crackled deafeningly and the electric-blue light that made up its grid formation flashed spectacularly. In an instant, Dawn and Dawn were gone.

9

fizz's mission

Hobey came to a skidding stop just the other side of the colourful cloud mass and proceeded to flip Fizz off her back. She hit the ground with a dull thud and watched as Hobey gave her a sly wink, then scampered away onto the other side of the cloud again.

"Welcome!" a voice boomed all around Fizz. She jumped to her feet and began looking around for the owner of the voice, but there was no one to be seen.

This side of the cloud was different. In front of her, Fizz found herself staring out into the infinite blackness of space.

It was beautiful.

It was as if she were standing on a cliff edge but, instead of gazing over endless miles of ocean, she was staring out at the Galaxy in all its infinite glory. Beneath her, she noticed that she was standing on a grid of electric-blue light – the Space-Time Vortex.

"Are you the Galaxy Guide?" the voice boomed out again. Fizz still couldn't see anyone around, but she answered anyway.

"Uh … yeah, if you want me to be!" she called out. "But if that's any reason to get in trouble or put me in danger then … no, I'm not the Galaxy Guide!"

Suddenly, the swirling mass of coloured cloud Fizz had just passed through began shifting and changing form again. It seemed to become solid and slowly, much to Fizz's amazement, it began to resemble … a face.

The face was as tall as a house. Not human: it looked almost … monstrous; its eyes were deep and sunken back into the cloud, its nose and mouth jagged and pointed as it leered at Fizz.

The mouth of this monstrous-looking face in the cloud began to open, letting out a deep, rumbling roar, and from inside Fizz spotted something – something rolling out of the mouth, something coming from within the cloud, something big … something metallic … something round. Instantly she recognised the shape and, while she was baffled as to how he had got here, Fizz felt a slight lift in her heart as she watched the familiar shape of Queeg rolling towards her.

Queeg rolled to a stop just in front of Fizz and his thin, spindly arms and legs shot out of his round body, shortly followed by his bizarrely-shaped head.

"Greetings, Galaxy Guide," he said with a cough. "Welcome to The Eye of the Galaxy. You must listen to Sarkon; my time for speaking is at an end. Listen carefully and ask no questions; Sarkon does not take kindly to being interrupted."

"Don't ask any questions!" Fizz snapped, angrily. "Time Tunnels! Missions! Giant squirrels! What the heck was *he* all about by the way? The Eye of the Galaxy, which, by the way, I didn't even know existed: and this bloke Sarkon! Who

does he think he is anyway? And why aren't you dead …
hmm? I saw you get killed!"

"I do not get … *killed*, as you put it," Queeg replied. "It is
virtually impossible to kill the Superintendent and Regulator
for the Space-Time Vortex."

"Well, who were those things I saw … big shadowy
things? They fired lasers; there was smoke, you were dying
…"

"SILENCE!" The giant face of Sarkon boomed. So
terrifying was his roar that Fizz actually went white with
fear.

"I told you," Queeg whispered. "Listen. Question time
will come soon enough."

"The Galaxy is doomed!" Sarkon began, as his face
expanded and contorted into various grave expressions, the
cloud shifting and its colours dimming like storm clouds.
"Tragedy has occurred and all things will perish."

"I don't like the sound of that," Fizz whispered. Queeg
glared at her, urging her to stay quiet.

"The Space-Time Vortex was never intended to be
disrupted; such disturbances will cause Galactic implosion.
I repeat … all things will perish."

"Does he have a point?" Fizz asked Queeg.

Before Queeg could tell Fizz to stay quiet, Sarkon lunged
forward; the now dark, gloomy clouds that made up his face
swirled and spun furiously as they encircled Fizz. Sarkon
roared with anger as his face disintegrated and changed into
a tornado of mist and fog.

Inside this spinning mass of cloud, Fizz curled herself into a ball and tried to ignore the images flashing all around her.

Planets zoomed around her head; flashes of the Space-Time Vortex crackled and hissed into view and disappeared again, over and over, like a light being flicked on and off. Fizz saw the people of Earth running and screaming with terror as the entire planet began to tip and tilt. She saw oceans rising and crashing over shores, trees uprooting themselves, other animals and creatures that inhabited the planet roaring with fear.

And then ... the cloud cleared, the images vanished and Fizz found herself once again standing next to Queeg and looking at the giant face of Sarkon in the clouds.

"Don't ... interrupt," Queeg said.

"Gotcha," Fizz replied, gasping and panting for breath. "Don't interrupt: good tip ... good tip." She looked up at Sarkon's enormous visage. "I'm all ears!" she shouted.

Sarkon continued.

"The Galactic disruption *must* be undone," Sarkon boomed. "Time *must* be set straight. The tragedy *must* be averted."

Fizz waited; she dared not say anything.

Seconds passed

Minutes passed.

Still Fizz didn't dare speak.

"SPEAK!" Sarkon bellowed.

"Oh, right," Fizz blurted out. "Oh, right, I can speak now? Right, okay ... umm ... well, I haven't got the foggiest what you're talking about."

Next to her, Fizz heard Queeg sighing despondently.

"What?!" she said, snapping her head round to face him. "Galactic disruption, Galactic implosion; I get all that, that's cool – the Galaxy's gonna destroy itself, okay? But ... what do you want *me* to do about it?"

"You must realign the timeline!" Sarkon replied, his giant face looming closer to Fizz.

"Oh, okay ..." Fizz said. "I'll get right on it, shall I? And just exactly how do I do that again? I mean, I haven't got my *time-realigning tools* on me at the moment."

Sarkon's enormous, sunken eyes shifted slightly in the cloud and looked at Queeg.

"She is dense, Superintendent," he said softly. "Must we entrust the future of every living being in the Galaxy to such a simple-minded creature?"

"Alas, your greatness, she is the only one," Queeg replied.

"Hang on a minute," Fizz protested. "Dense, am I? Simple-minded? Well, how about you two stop talking in flaming riddles and just tell me what's going on around here and what you want me to do about it? Talk to me straight and I'll tell you what I think I can do!"

Silence followed as Queeg and Sarkon stared at each other.

"Allow me, greatness," Queeg said.

"Very well," Sarkon replied, as his face shrunk back away from Fizz.

"Behold, Galaxy Guide," Queeg said, turning Fizz round and pointing out to the infinite Galaxy in front of them. Fizz now saw Earth floating in front of her. It was no longer green and blue; now it looked grey and brown, with patches of black.

"What you are looking at is the Earth as it is now," Queeg went on. "It is dead and every creature on it is extinct, including the human race."

"I knew this already," Fizz said.

"When a planet is relocated," Queeg went on, "and all of its inhabitants become extinct, the planet and the very memories of that planet and all its species cease to have ever existed; they are wiped from time. *Completely* from time."

"Okay," Fizz said.

"Unfortunately, your friend Dawn Gray has survived the relocation. She is the last surviving inhabitant of Earth and she is lost somewhere in time and space, and this ... is *bad*."

"Bad. Okay. And why is that?"

"The Earth was relocated. It does not exist any more, nor do any of its inhabitants. The Space-Time Vortex knows this and yet, for some reason it cannot explain, it detects a human life-form existing somewhere in time and it is becoming confused ... disrupted. The Vortex knows that humans should never have existed, that they have been wiped from time and space, that nobody should ever have heard of them. But there is still a human, an Earthling, wandering around space and time. This Earthling, this human, this ... Dawn Gray, has nowhere to go, no planet to live on. The Vortex does not know what to do with her, where to put her. Eventually it will become so confused, so disrupted that it will just give up and collapse, and when the

Space-Time Vortex collapses … the Galaxy will destroy itself and implode."

"I've heard all this before," Fizz said. "From the Empress Garcea." Queeg looked nervously at Sarkon upon hearing the Empress's name. Fizz did not notice their acknowledged looks of concern. "I tried to go back," Fizz said. "Tried to DROSS Dawn off the Earth before it was towed away and get her and her parents to Squetania Blib, where they could start a new life, but …"

"Something went wrong, yes?" Queeg finished.

"That's when I met you."

"Time will keep repeating itself, Galaxy Guide," Queeg said. "That's what time does when there is a problem, a glitch in the Space-Time Vortex. The Earth, as far as the Vortex is concerned, has been wiped from time; it does not exist. However, all the while an Earthling exists in time and space, the memory of the Earth will go on and time will repeat itself over and over and over again, until the Vortex can take no more."

"So what do we do?" Fizz asked. "What do you want me to do?"

"You must find Dawn Gray," Queeg replied. "You must find her and you must both travel back to the moment the Earth was about to be towed."

"And make sure we DROSS off and evacuate to Squetania Blib this time?" Fizz asked.

Queeg looked at Sarkon again.

"NO!" Sarkon boomed, making Fizz jump. "You must not go to Squetania Blib."

"But that's where all evacuees go when their home planets are relocated. That's what Galaxy Guides do. That's what The Galactic Association for Galaxy Guides, Universal Transporters and LX Travellers does – it saves as many beings as it can from being wiped out in planet relocations."

"You could take Dawn and her parents to Squetania Blib," Queeg said. "That would set time straight; that would save the Earth girl and her mother and father, but ..."

"But what?" Fizz asked.

Queeg suddenly looked nervous. He shuffled his spindly legs anxiously, his round, metal body wobbling as he did so.

"But *what*?" Fizz pushed.

"The Galactic Council's order to relocate the Earth was ..." – Queeg seemed to pause for dramatic effect – "*illegal*," he finally finished.

"Illegal? After the way the human race treated their planet? The Interstellar Bill of Harmonious Law and Rights was written for human beings. I quote ..." Fizz cleared her throat – "Any being found guilty of not living peacefully with other beings or found guilty of destroying their planet risks incurring the penalty of planet relocation.

"Isn't that right? I had to learn that for my Galaxy Guide exam, by the way; we had to know the Interstellar Bill of Harmonious Law and Rights off by heart. I got an A."

Queeg nodded.

"It is true: the human race is hated throughout the Galaxy and if humans were the only species on Earth, they would have been relocated and left to rot at the dark end of the Galaxy for they way they treated the Earth. However, they are not the only species on Earth and, the truth is, many innocent life forms are now extinct on the surface of the dead Earth and they should not be."

A sudden realisation swept through Fizz; she wasn't sure she wanted to hear the answer to her next question but, nevertheless, it was a question she had to ask.

"What do you want me and Dawn to do?" she said.

Queeg hesitated, looking at Sarkon for support.

"Tell her," Sarkon boomed.

"We don't want you to go back in time and save the Earth girl Dawn Gray," Queeg said. "We want the two of you to go back in time and … save the Earth itself."

10

mantor's rebirth

Once, he had been a terrifying, mysterious figure known throughout the Galaxy as Mantor. Many believed him to be only a myth, a legend – a kind of Galactic bogeyman.

Once, he had lived as long as the Galaxy had existed, created by a mother who had only one use in mind for him: to maintain control of time and space throughout the Galaxy and in every pocket of the Space-Time Vortex.

Once, he had travelled billions of light years, through countless dimensions, across space and time and into the terrifying, unknown reaches of space, further than any living creature had ever been able or had ever dared to venture.

And then … one fateful day, this monstrous guardian was …

… flattened by a gigantic, squelching, gelatinous blob.

Mantor had pursued, in fact hunted, Fizz and Dawn across time and across dimensions when the pair had inadvertently altered time by escaping the Earth as it had been towed.

The three of them were trapped within the Space-Time Vortex. The two girls were at his mercy and then, from nowhere, a creature called Jowlox the One had descended upon Mantor from above like a blancmange the size of a house.

Mantor had stood no chance.

Time, for Mantor, had stopped there and then. For Jowlox too, time, space and the Galaxy itself all seemed to cease moving; after all, he had killed the guardian of the Space-Time Vortex. When time stopped for Mantor, it stopped for anyone close to him as well.

And yet now – as time went on in all its different dimensions, as Dawn and Dawn tried to escape the planet they were trapped on, as Fizz fell deeper and deeper into an adventure she had absolutely no desire to get involved in – time, for Mantor and Jowlox continued, albeit cut off from the rest of the Galaxy.

It was called a Time Pocket: not the most common occurrence in Galactic time and space, but one a few beings are aware of. Time Pockets are rifts in time: breaks, tears, rips, where whatever beings were in the pocket at the moment it was formed can remain safe and sound, cut off from the rest of time and space.

In the cargo hold aboard the Trygonian Council Recovery Vessel, Jowlox wriggled and giggled with delight. Immediately, he began shape-shifting to try and imitate the physical appearance of the armour-clad being he had so unceremoniously squashed.

Jowlox was the last of a species known as Mimicaabus. The Mimicaabus, or Mimicaabi, are able to alter their DNA code to replicate the appearance of another being or, for that matter, a physical emotion. Jowlox, in his present slobbering, drooling, blob-like state, was the living, oozing interpretation of a hug – a manifestation he thought quite desirable in order to convince humanoid beings to become his friend. Needless to say, when Fizz and Dawn had encountered Jowlox's 'hug', the last thing they had wanted to do was embrace it.

Finally, after some minutes, Jowlox achieved his goal and replicated Mantor's appearance.

He stood himself up and examined himself thoroughly. He had grown to nearly eight feet tall and was clad in shiny, plate-like armour that looked like human flesh. About his body was a vast array of tools and weapons, all secured around his waist. He was wrapped in dark but fresh-looking bandages, a bit like a mummy. As he reached his hands up to his face and head, Jowlox instantly realised the need for the bandages: they were to disguise his appearance.

He did not have a head.

He did not have a face.

Instead, all there was on top of his shoulders was a shiny black skull, wrapped in some smooth, metallic-looking, black material. In the centre of this smooth, solid, black skull, where the face should have been, was a blank screen.

The bandages hung loosely around Jowlox's head, partially hiding his new and bizarre appearance, but nevertheless the blank screen where his face should have been was quite unmistakable.

Jowlox looked down at the motionless focus of his latest replication.

The original Mantor looked exactly the same as Jowlox, only a hundred, maybe a thousand years older, which of course he probably was.

His blank screen was cracked, his armour faded, battered and covered in laser blasts and burns. His bandages were torn and ripped, caked with dried blood of many colours.

This Mantor was old and defeated.

Jowlox was a new, shiny, stronger Mantor.

The only thing Jowlox didn't have was the original Mantor's memory banks. He didn't know what Mantor knew; he hadn't seen what Mantor had seen and he didn't have the compelling, overwhelming urge to hunt down and kill anyone who disrupted the Space–Time Vortex.

No, Jowlox was exactly like Mantor to look at – but that was all.

As Jowlox stood, trying to figure out whether he liked his new look or not, Mantor's fingers twitched.

His hand moved, but Jowlox didn't notice.

It wasn't until Mantor's blank screen suddenly clicked on and a luminous green message ran across it, that Jowlox suddenly realised he was in big trouble.

I AM MANTOR

the message ran.

Instantly, Jowlox's screen flickered to life and Mantor reached up with his exhausted, half-mechanical, half-organic arm and grabbed his replica by the throat with such force that Jowlox found he could no longer breathe.

Mantor dragged Jowlox to his knees and pulled his head towards his own until both Mantors – both blank screens, both black skulls – were pressed against each other.

I AM MANTOR

the message on Mantor's screen ran again.

I WILL TERMINATE IN
T-MINUS 60 SECONDS

Jowlox began to struggle and fight against Mantor's grasp, but it was no use; Mantor was too strong and Jowlox could not break away. As he tried to shape-shift into a different form, Mantor squeezed his clawed hand tighter around his throat and Jowlox squealed with pain; he lost his concentration and his shape-shift failed.

He was stuck as Mantor for now.

YOU MUST LEARN

A new message appeared on Mantor's screen, a message Jowlox didn't much like the look of.

I HAVE MUCH TO TEACH

YOU MUST LEARN

Suddenly, Jowlox began shaking and convulsing violently as a stream of digital data began flowing from Mantor's screen into his own.

Every bit of data, everything Mantor had been taught and learned over millions of years exploring the Galaxy, flashed from his screen into Jowlox's, into the new Mantor … into the new, stronger, faster Mantor.

Jowlox wailed and screamed, but it was useless to resist.

After just a single minute, both screens went black and Mantor collapsed to the floor, laid on his back, motionless, his screen blank: dead.

Towering above him, his flesh-like armour shining even in the gloom of the poorly lit cargo hold, stood a figure, tall and ominous.

The figure wrapped its bandages tightly around its head and arms, straightening its claw-like fingers, cracking the knuckles and flexing the muscles.

The figure was silent, the figure was motionless – but through the bandages a message could be seen in green writing, flickering faintly behind the bandages.

I AM MANTOR

11

a change of luck?

It was a peculiar sensation, being tossed around through time and space. Dawn, of course, had experienced it before, and at the time she thought she would never forget the feeling of stepping into the Space-Time Vortex and feeling nothing but empty Galaxy all around her.

But as she and her unluckier namesake vanished from the planet they had thought they would be stranded on forever and found themselves, instead, standing amongst a cheering and applauding audience, Dawn suddenly realised that she had completely forgotten what it was like to travel billions of light years in the blink of an eye.

"Do we go?" the other Dawn Gray asked, nervously.

Dawn looked around her quickly. She couldn't take in too much, but she saw bright lights and she heard cheering voices and laughter all around her and immediately thought:

This ll do.

"Run!" she screamed, as she grabbed the other Dawn by the hand and dragged her as far away from the spot they had been standing on as quickly as she could.

Behind the two Dawns, the Vortex crackled and hissed and vanished in another flash of electric-blue light. The two girls came to a stop, panting and clasping each other.

"What … just … happened?" the other Dawn asked.

Dawn smiled and patted her new friend on the shoulder.

"We just escaped from planet Dawn Gray," she said. "The Vortex tried to relocate us here, for whatever reason, but before it had time to realise that we don't belong here, we made a run for it. When the Vortex zapped that pocket of space and time back to where we came from, we weren't in it any more."

"Oh," the other Dawn said, a little puzzled. "Right."

"I'm just glad we found somewhere obviously happy and full of friendly people first time. We could have been zapping backwards and forwards for years finding somewhere safe to get out to."

"Maybe my luck's changing after all," the other Dawn Gray said, smiling and feeling thoroughly pleased with herself.

The two girls smiled and hugged each other – and at that very same moment, a giant cage dropped from the sky above them, trapping them inside.

12

orlak the great

The cage appeared to be made of light. Dozens of vertical bars towered up above the two girls; the bars glowed a bright, luminous-green. Dawn reached out and touched one of the bars; it crackled and fizzed, making Dawn pull her hand away in shock.

The laughter and cheers all around them grew louder and louder, and then the applause started. The light was so bright that neither Dawn could see beyond the cage, but both were sure that that they were surrounded by hundreds of people.

Dawn and Dawn clung tightly on to each other, squinting into the bright light, trying to see who was around them and where they were.

Suddenly the cage seemed to lift off the ground and, surprisingly, the two girls were lifted with it. The cage, Dawn and Dawn moved forwards and the bright light around them began to fade. The voices and the cheering faded as well until, after just a minute or two, the girls were carried into eerie, quiet darkness.

The cage was set back down on rough, uneven ground.

There was the sound of a door being slammed shut and then there was just silence. Silence, darkness and the eerie, dim glow of the bars that held them prisoner.

"What just happened?" Dawn said, more to herself than to her unlucky double.

"I'm not sure," the other Dawn replied. "But I do know that my luck hasn't changed after all."

Dawn suddenly felt a twinge of pity for her alternative self. She thought for a moment about saying something to comfort her, something to help her feel that this situation was not her fault; but somewhere in the back of her mind, as much as she hated to admit it, Dawn couldn't help feeling that this stroke of what seemed to be disastrous luck had been brought on by the unluckiest Dawn Gray alive in the Galaxy.

Dawn dismissed the thought immediately, refusing to allow herself to dwell on such ridiculous paranoia.

Suddenly, sounds came from out of the darkness.

They were not alone. As their eyes began to focus and become accustomed to the darkness, the girls realised that theirs was not the only cage in the room. All around them were dozens of other brightly-lit cages. They could not see the occupants of these cages, but judging by the various unpleasant sounds of growls, scurryings and moans, they guessed that they were not in entirely friendly company.

"There's something in here with us," the other Dawn whispered. There was a definite note of panic in her trembling voice. Dawn, on the other hand, was surprisingly calm. She had been in worse spots before now – chased by savage, mutant bulldogs and facing complete and total extermination at the hands of that thing called Mantor - so that so far this situation was nothing more than very intriguing, albeit slightly unnerving.

Unfortunately, it was about to get a whole lot worse.

The door that had been slammed shut just a few minutes earlier suddenly swung open again and a tall, freakishly-thin figure crept silently into the room.

The figure seemed to be dressed in some sort of long coat, or cloak, which dragged along the ground behind him. But the limbs that this garment covered were unnaturally thin; its skeletal arms and legs were twice as long as they should have been.

The figure carried a lantern held aloft in its bony hand. It was wearing some kind of beaten-up, dishevelled top hat, but beneath it Dawn could not see its face in the gloom.

The figure in the top hat crept further into the room, moving slowly and tentatively, almost as a spider does, each leg seeming to test the ground beneath it as it stepped.

The movement in the cages around Dawn and Dawn became more frantic. Whatever the creatures or beings in the cages were, they were not pleased to see this creepy, spindly-looking figure, and the further into the room it came, the more frenzied became the movement in the other cages. The low growls and moans turned into anxious, frightened whines and whimpers and, just a few inches from the two Dawns' cage, the tall figure stopped and peered around the room, holding its lantern higher.

"Nak-Taa!" the figure hissed, in a voice so menacing it made Dawn's and Dawn's blood run cold. "NAK-TAA!" it bellowed again, and this time the room fell deathly silent.

The figure turned back to the cage the two Dawns were in and peered through the bars, circling it like some kind of hideous predator.

It was grotesque.

Both girls recoiled in horror as its thin, bony, hairy face squeezed in between two of the bars. It was white, bone-white, but all around it was thick, coarse, black hair. From inside its thin-lipped mouth two fangs protruded, and its eyes were shiny and black like marbles. When it blinked, several pairs of eyelids fluttered down and then rolled up again. It was quite monstrous. It looked like a big, thin, walking, talking … bug.

"Nak-tillia?" it hissed teasingly thought the bars. "Nak-Portaar, Nik?"

Dawn and Dawn peered back at the horrific face beneath the top hat.

"We … don't understand," Dawn mumbled, through trembling lips.

"Ah … Earthish, yes?" the bug-like creature whispered, smiling and baring its long fangs. "Very well. I am Orlak the Great, Ringmaster of Spectalica-Galactica, or, if you prefer in your own language, The Galaxy Spectacle."

"Ringmaster?" Dawn echoed. "This is … a circus?"

"I don't know where you came from," Orlak went on, ignoring Dawn. "And I'm not sure how you appeared in the middle of a show tonight, but you two Earthlings have just made me a lot of Daktaa and I like making lots of Daktaa."

"Daktaa?" Dawn repeated again. "Is that … *money*?"

"Daktaa is Universal Trading Credit," Orlak hissed in reply. "Daktaa is the currency of the Galaxy. It can be traded for anything you wish. Every species in the Galaxy nowadays speaks and deals only in Daktaa." Orlak smiled thinly again and sucked air through his teeth. "I like Daktaa."

The two girls held tightly onto each other's hands and Dawn stepped forward, closer to the bars, closer to Orlak.

"Mr … Orlak, sir," she muttered, nervously. "I think there's been a horrible mistake."

Orlak pushed his head further into through the bars; his black, marble-like eyes narrowed slightly as he stared right at Dawn.

"We … er …" – Dawn wasn't quite sure how to put it. "We didn't mean to come here. We … dimension-hopped, you see? Through the Space-Time Vortex. We're not really performers, you know? I mean, my friend here isn't a clown and I'm no trapeze artist." She laughed nervously, as Orlak glared at her. "So, we'd be no good to you in your circus. You understand what it's like in the Galaxy and all that, don't you? You know, you dimension-hop here, dimension-hop there. If you'd let us go now, we could just find our way out and …"

"We leave for Grakonia tonight," Orlak said, almost as though Dawn wasn't even talking. "We have two shows on Grakonia and you two are going to be the headline act!"

"No, wait!" Dawn said, beginning to panic. "You don't understand! We shouldn't be here! This is wrong! All wrong!"

Orlak began to chuckle to himself as he turned to leave, his lantern held up, leading his way out of the dark room.

"Wait!" Dawn screamed again. "Neither of us can juggle, you know!"

At the doorway, Orlak turned back.

"No need for party tricks in Spectalica-Galactica," he said, softly. "This is not a performing show."

Dawn stared back at Orlak in confusion.

"What kind of show is this?"

"It is my little freak show!" Orlak bellowed, triumphantly. "We have species from all over the Galaxy in Spectalica-Galactica. Some of the rarest creatures and beings in existence, some that are the last of their kind … like you."

"Like … us?" Dawn said.

"Earthlings don't exist any more, child. And I have found two, probably the last two Earthlings alive. Do you know how much Daktaa people will trade just to come and stare at you? Just to come and stare at the most universally-hated species in the Galaxy? Everyone hates Earthlings and everyone was glad when the Earth was relocated, but everyone will want to come and stare at you, mock you, jeer at you, throw things at you. And everyone will trade handsomely to do so. Oh yes, tonight will be the greatest triumph in Spectalica-Galactica history. You two … are going to be legends."

Orlak continued to chuckle to himself as he left the room.

In their cage, back in darkness, the two Dawn Grays fell into each other's arms and began to cry.

13

an unexpected reunion

There were, of course, one or two questions that sprang to Fizz's mind. Being told that you have to travel back in time and save the entire Galaxy and zillions of life forms from certain death poses a few questions that one would like clarified: not least of which, how exactly do you go about doing just that?

Fizz however chose to ignore these pressing concerns and, instead, as she walked with Queeg through what seemed to be an endless maze of tunnels and corridors, with Queeg's motors and mechanical drivers humming gently as he rolled along beside her, she brought up the subject of Hobey again.

"So what's with the giant, freaky squirrel?"

"Hobey? Hobey is a Time Pocket Mutation," Queeg replied, as he wobbled alongside Fizz, still coughing and spluttering.

"Oh … right," Fizz said. "And that is …?"

"Occasionally, creatures and beings get caught in pockets of time, called Time Pockets, which are lapses in the Space-Time Vortex. They are moments of time that are lost or miscalculated as the Vortex shifts or changes for some reason. Creatures from all over the Galaxy, from many different worlds, are suddenly and inexplicably zapped into thin air. It happened on Earth: look up the mystery of a chap called Glenn Miller. And who on Earth ever found out why things really disappeared in the Bermuda Triangle, hmm?"

"So ..." Fizz wondered. "Why is he the size of an elephant?"

"Oh, that's just part of the mutation. When creatures are lost in Time Pockets they sometimes change shape or size, act differently, speak differently. Hobey mutated as he travelled through gaps in the Vortex, and ended up in The Eye of the Galaxy, which was a zillion-to-one chance. His DNA make-up was completely altered and he found himself with the ability to communicate. He's a completely unique species, but he does still have a weakness for nuts."

"Yeah, so I saw," Fizz replied. "And where exactly do the nuts come from?"

"The same Time Pocket," Queeg replied. "Once a Time Pocket has been formed in the Vortex, there it remains ... Luckily for Hobey, the occasional nut rolls into the Pocket and falls through to him." Queeg coughed again and wheezed as he caught his breath. "Actually, you have come very close to being lost in a Time Pocket yourself, young Galaxy Guide," Queeg went on.

"Really?"

"Indeed. On my travels, I happened to come across a rather interesting little fellow I think you know quite well. I have decided to reintroduce the pair of you. Between you, you managed to find Dawn Gray before; it is my hope that this time the two of you, working together, will have the same kind of success with this mission."

The endless, dark tunnel came to an end and Fizz found herself standing in front of a giant, steel door.

"I must warn you, however," Queeg went on. "Your friend is a little different from how you might remember him."

Queeg pushed a button on the wall and the steel door zipped up. Behind it was a small, dull room with another door on the other side. In the centre of the room was a table, upon which several items were scattered and there, hovering just a few feet off the ground, was the strangest, oddest-looking robot Fizz had ever seen.

"Wemember me?" the little robot chirped.

"Kevin?" Fizz said, disbelievingly.

"That's wight; you do wemember me! How do you like my new look?"

The last time Fizz had seen Kevin he had been a little silver, rugby ball-shaped robot with the most vivid blue eyes. When Fizz first encountered him, he had been the happiest little machine anyone could have ever met, completely and utterly incapable of being offended. During their time together and their chase across the Galaxy to save Dawn, however, he had grown to be a little ... well, moody to say the least. But now ... now Kevin was *really* different.

For a start he had a tail.

Yes, you read right: he had a tail. And not a shiny, silver attachment on his backside to match the rest of his body. Oh no; now Kevin had a furry, brown, wagging tail.

And ears.

Yes ... ears. They matched his tail, at least, which was some consolation, but nevertheless the rest of Kevin was shiny and silver and rugby ball-shaped, which made him the most bizarre thing Fizz had ever seen.

"You look like a freak," Fizz said bluntly. "Why aren't you dead?"

"Oh, charming!" Kevin said. "Weally nice to see you too, mate. It's nice to see you haven't lost any of your charm."

Fizz couldn't help smiling.

"It's good to see you, Kev," she said.

"Off to find Dawn Gway again, then?" Kevin replied, smiling back at Fizz, his little pale blue eyes flashing brightly.

"I'll kill her when I find her," Fizz replied. "The saviour of the Galaxy had to be the pain in my bum, didn't it?"

14

---

the galactic council convenes

The message had been faint and slightly jumbled, but there was no doubt who it was from.

AWAITING COORDINATES

SPACE-TIME VORTEX UNSTABLE

UNIDENTIFIED LIFE-FORM PRESENT

AWAITING COORDINATES

The message had been transmitted from a Time Pocket somewhere. A newly formed Time Pocket, one the Galactic Council was not aware of.

A meeting was called immediately.

Empress Garcea floated gracefully, but not without a sense of urgency, through the magnificent, brightly-lit hallways of the Galactic Council's headquarters, hidden away on the mountain planet of Everesta 9.

Once, Empress Garcea had been a new and frowned-upon member of the Galactic Council. Until her appointment, only purely organic life forms had been allowed to occupy Council seats and the mere thought of a Luminious life-form from planet Grahl taking any kind of place in the Galactic Council had been nothing more than an outrageous joke, and not a very funny one at that.

Luminious life-forms, for those of you who do not know, are living cells held together not by skin, bones and internal organs but instead by complicated fields of light. This light is an organic form of light which emits from the Luminious being's only solid bodily organ … the BirthHeart.

The BirthHeart is what the female Luminious life-forms give birth to at the end of their term of pregnancy, which by the way is 71 years, 3 months and 17 days. The, tiny, banana-shaped BirthHeart is then nurtured and loved, kept warm and safe. After a time, the BirthHeart begins to emit different rays of light which, after many more years, form a new, unique and individual Luminious life-form, or Luminiae.

Not purely organic.

A presence defined purely by light around a single organic organ.

Empress Garcea and her fellow Grahlanians were considered, for many light years, to be a 'subspecies', not worthy of any place of authority and certainly not of any seat on the Galactic Council.

Empress Garcea had never been truly welcomed at the Galactic Council. Now, however … *now*, things were very different. Now, Empress Garcea *was* the Galactic Council.

"Is the Council assembled?" the Empress asked in her light, almost melodious tone, with her six fluttering eyes flitting above her mysterious veil. Behind her, Jevkaa Creebo walked tall and proud, as he always did when he was in his Mistress' presence.

"They are, Highness," he replied, bowing. "And they await your arrival."

"Good," the Empress said. "My baby lives and they must all know that I intend to finish what I began. And Jevkaa ..." Empress Garcea suddenly added, turning back to her faithful servant. Jevkaa looked at his Mistress expectantly.

Jevkaa Creebo, unlike the Mistress he so faithfully served, was completely organic and was a Tendall life form, a being created and bred for the sole purpose of serving those who employed him. Jevkaa Creebo, however, was more than a Tendall to Empress Garcea. Living and working with the Garcea Dynasty for more than seven hundred years, Jevkaa had become family, a confidant for Empress Garcea, a friend – perhaps her best friend: a being who would die for his Mistress, no matter what the cost.

Empress Garcea studied Jevkaa for a moment. His long, shiny gown was fastened up to his chin and his metallic-looking face was a fixed, grim expression of consolation.

"I don't like that face, Jevkaa," the Empress snapped. "It depresses me. Change it."

In an instant, several different expressions melted on and off Jevkaa's Liquisage – or skull, to you and me. The gel-like liquid that made up his physical, facial appearance, altering and sculpting itself to make a new and more pleasing visage for the Empress to look upon.

Finally, the gel-like liquid contained behind the clear plastic front of Jevkaa's Liquisage settled and set. His new expression was a happier one, though it still appeared concerned and thoughtful.

"That's better," the Empress said. "Now, let us address the Council and inform them of the wonderful news. Mantor is alive and Earth, finally, will be wiped from history for good."

15

grakons and grakonia

When Spectalica-Galactica comes to your planet, you know about it. A hundred times longer than a Trygonian Recovery Vessel and a mile wide, you couldn't help but notice when the travelling circus came into orbit and began its descent towards your home planet's surface.

Of course, it was all highly illegal: it couldn't possibly be anything but. I mean, a travelling show, charging ridiculous trading prices to come and stare at some of the rarest, most sought-after beings in the history of the Galaxy, some of which should actually be extinct ...

The Galactic Council had known about Spectalica-Galactica since it began its business, but the truth was that the Galactic Council didn't care. It was far too busy relocating planets, wiping out entire races, civilisations and species, to worry about the odd travelling freak-show rumbling around space and earning a slightly dishonest living.

And the visitors to Spectalica-Galactica? Shouldn't they have complained about the show trading illegally? Reported them? Boycotted it? No, of course not. For one thing, who would anyone complain to? If the Galactic Council didn't care, nobody cared. And anyway, the truth was, illegal or not, everyone loved Spectalica-Galactica. Where else would they get the chance, no matter how much it cost them, to look at some of the rarest beings in existence, beings they wouldn't otherwise ever get the chance of seeing? No, even though it was illegal and immoral, Spectalica-Galactica was never going to go out of business, because everyone loved it.

The planet Grakonia was no different.

Grakonia was not much more than a big swamp. It was about as far away from any heat, from any star, anywhere in the Galaxy, as you could get. That meant, therefore, that it was a gloomy, dark and damp place. Four moons orbited Grakonia, and the planet's ecosystem thrived on moisture and shade, which basically meant that Grakonia was a giant swampland, overgrown with wild plants, trees and foliage.

The Grakons themselves had, over time, adapted to their harsh, inhospitable environment. At least, most of them had.

For many years now, a small civil unrest had begun to escalate among the Grakon people: a civil unrest between the Aquakon Grakons and the Terra Firmakon Grakons. The Aquakons were the Grakon elders, who still believed that the Grakon race was an aquatic race born and bred in the swamplands, and that it was in the swamplands of Grakonia they should stay. The Terra Firmakons, on the other hand, were the new breed of progressive Grakons who had chosen to leave the swampland and learn to live, breathe and survive on land. Terra Firmakons believed that for the Grakon race to survive, it should learn to exist outside the swampland.

But in the end, be they Aquakons or Terra Firmakons, all Grakons were essentially the same. Bizarre, scaly creatures that sported gills and flippers to help them breathe and move about their swampland home. In fact, the Grakons were so well adapted to their damp, unwelcoming world that they were simply unable to exist anywhere else – anywhere where there was sunlight or heat, or a lack of moisture in the air.

The only things the Grakons did have in abundance, other than mud, grime and dark, gloomy swampland, was Daktaa. The ways and means by which the Grakons came into so much credit is best left unexplained; suffice it to say that it involved hijacking ships that flew too close to Grakon, a smidgen of tinkering with engines, and outrageous charges for fixing the engines so that ships and their crews could get off Grakon as quickly as possible.

So you have a species living on an inhospitable world it cannot leave and, therefore, never seeing any other being. A world so hostile that no other being would ever dare to go near it. This same species, however, has an abundance of Daktaa, the Universal Trading Credit.

It's not hard to see why Orlak, the owner and ringleader of Spectalica-Galactica, loved visiting Grakonia and why the Grakons loved it when Spectalica-Galactica came to their planet.

16

zak

The Spectalica-Galactica landed, not with a dull thud or a crunch, but with a kind of squelching, sinking feeling.

In the Performers' Confinement Zone, Dawn and Dawn were jolted awake by the sound of engines hissing and brakes squealing.

"We've landed," Dawn said, sitting up straight and shuffling to the bars of the cage, which were still flickering brightly in the darkness of the Confinement Zone.

"Grakonia, I suppose," the other Dawn muttered, shivering. "Dawn? What's going to happen?"

"I don't know," Dawn replied. "I really don't know."

"You're gonna be humiliated, spat at, leered at and jeered at," a voice came from the darkness. "Then you're gonna be brought back here, thrown back in your cage and given a rusty bowl full of raw, diced Yalabya Sand Critter to eat and told to wait until Spectalica-Galactica arrives at its next venue."

Dawn and Dawn peered through the darkness, past the other cages scattered all around them, to one particular cage that was standing alone in the corner of the Confinement

Zone. This cage was different from all the other cages. Instead of glowing beams of light, the bars of this cage seemed to be solid metal. The figure behind the bars was crouched down, pressed against the frame of its prison.

"It's gonna be horrible; you're gonna hate it."

"Shut up," Dawn snapped. "Who are you?"

"Me?" The figure replied. "My name's Zak; pleased to meet you. Welcome to the worst spot in the Galaxy. Hope you enjoy your stay."

Dawn's unlucky alternative self came closer to the bars, squinting to see the figure on the opposite side of the dark room a little better.

"Why are your bars solid?" she asked. "Why aren't they made of ..."

"Light?" Zak finished. "I'll show you."

What happened next was so completely and utterly disturbing and freaky to witness that to say Dawn and Dawn were frozen with terror would be the biggest understatement since Horath Yackleput, the famous scientist who first discovered the infiniteness of space, uttered the phrase: "*This Galaxy thing: big, innit?*"

Dawn and Dawn could only watch in amazement as Zak's left arm cracked, squeaked and clicked, unhinged itself and extended through the solid bars, across the floor of the Confinement Zone all the way across to their cage. Dawn dared a closer look at Zak's hand as it hovered in front of the flickering beams of light that held her captive. His hand was ... well, not exactly a hand; it was more like a little Swiss army knife. It had all kinds of funny-looking devices sticking out all over it; some lit up, some flashed different-coloured lights, some had weird-looking screwdriver attachments. As

Zak held his hand out and turned it over so it was – well, so it was what should have been palm up, the two girls watched in astonishment as the metal-looking blades where his fingers should have been, and which had all the funny-looking attachments sticking out of them, suddenly fanned out to make a kind of metallic-looking webbed hand. Zak slipped the hand into the fields of green light and instantly, the energy field broken, the bars vanished.

"See?" Zak said, proudly. "Light-bars are no good for me. You can escape now, by the way, if you want to."

Dawn and Dawn looked at each other.

"Where would we go?" Dawn said.

"Well, that's the problem, isn't it?" Zak replied, cockily. "You could get out of the cage now as easily as you could walk through an open door, but getting out of the Confinement Zone is a lot harder. Getting out of Spectalica-Galactica without Orlak seeing you: very difficult. And getting off Grakonia, now … well, that's just impossible."

Zak removed his hand and the beams of green light shot back up, trapping the two Dawns inside their cage again. A series of rather painful-sounding clicks and cracks snapped through the darkness as Zak's arm retracted, back across the room, through the solid bars of his own cage and snugly back into his shoulder socket where it should have been, neatly back to a comfortable-looking length.

"You're mean," the other Dawn Gray said.

"You are," Dawn agreed. "Why would you do that to us – show us a way to get out of the cage like that when you know full well we can't go anywhere?"

"Just a little taster of what I can do," Zak replied, slouching down and sitting back against his bars. "And anyway, you asked."

"Have you ever tried to escape?" Dawn asked.

"Lots of times," Zak replied. "Reckon I found a way to do it as well."

"Then why haven't you?"

"Because Orlak came up with the idea of putting me behind solid bars before I could put my plan into effect," Zak replied.

"So you can escape Spectalica-Galactica, but you can't get out of your cage?" Dawn said.

"'Bout the size of it, yeah. I need someone who's willing to escape with me, to help me get out of this thing. If I can get out of this cage, I can get whoever helps me out of Spectalica-Galactica and off most rocks."

"Most rocks?" the other Dawn repeated.

"You can't escape Grakonia," Zak said. "Too isolated. We're in the depths of the Galaxy out here, you know. Get me onto solid terrain, a planet nearer civilised space, and I got my ways."

Dawn and Dawn looked at each other.

"We'll help you," they said together. Zak turned and, although the two girls couldn't see it through the darkness, he smiled at them both.

"After the show," he said. "We'll talk more after the show."

"After the show?" Dawn said, a nervous tremble in her voice. "Why ... after the show?"

"Orlak's coming," Zak said. "It's show time."

17

fizz gets her answers

On the table between Fizz and Kevin were four items. The first item was a Locator-Sphere, a device Fizz had used before. A Locator-Sphere tracks and locates an individual being within the Galaxy, as well as every other alternative version of that being in every other possible dimension.

The second item on the table Fizz also recognised; it was a Time Tunnel. She had seen Queeg use a Time Tunnel when they had first met.

The other two items Fizz did not recognise; one was a little black box that looked a bit like an MP3 player, while the other was a clear plastic tray containing what looked like five small, transparent eggs.

"Very well then," Queeg coughed. "Reintroductions finished with, let us get on to our assignment, shall we? There isn't much time."

"Stop!" Fizz suddenly bellowed. "Hang on a minute. I'm not happy with any of this, Queegy."

"Excuse me?" Queeg said.

"Oh, here we go," Kevin said tutting. "You weally never learn when to keep that mouth of yours shut, do you?"

"I have a few questions, if that's okay with everyone," Fizz went on, folding her arms in an unflappable stance of defiance. "All I ever hear from you is … *there isn t much time; ooh, dear me, Galaxy Guide, there isn t much time, the Galaxy will be destroyed soon; there isn t much time*. Well *knickers* to time! You want me to save the Earth? Risk my neck, go hopping about space and time … *again*! To find Dawn Gray … *again*? You'd better just find a bit of *precious time* and answer my questions, get it?"

There was a moment's silence. Fizz panted heavily; Kevin watched her nervously as a faint trace of smoke began to waft out of her left ear.

Queeg watched Fizz with a look of interest all of a sudden. His legs retracted slowly and his large, round body eased to the floor where it wobbled gently back and forth.

"You are a *Temper*Tantrumous?"

Fizz huffed and puffed and caught her breath.

"Yeah," she replied. "I blow up when I get too angry … literally. So unless you want a big, gaping hole in the middle of The Eye of the Galaxy, and unless you really, *really* wanna test that theory that Superintendents of the Space-Time Vortex can't be killed … I suggest you tell me what I wanna know."

Queeg seemed to smile at Fizz.

"I like you, Galaxy Guide," he said, fondly. "You have courage. Courage and a respect for life that perhaps you do not understand or even know you have. Ask away … I will answer your questions."

Fizz hopped up onto the table, shoving the rather delicate and expensive-looking objects aside, and crossed her legs.

"First off …" she began. "What the heck is GOING ON??!!"

Kevin reeled back, spinning away from Fizz as she bellowed. Queeg, however, did not flinch; he simply gazed at Fizz with a fixed expression of kindness and admiration.

"I'm afraid I do not understand the question, Galaxy Guide. I thought Sarkon and myself had explained the situation quite clearly to you. Which bit in particular do you not understand?"

"Well now, let me see," Fizz said, scratching her head. "The bit about me racing through space and time and across the Galaxy to save a planet that's already dead and a species that, in all honesty, deserves to be wiped out. That bit really. I just need you to clear up exactly why I'm doing this again."

"Why did you become a Galaxy Guide?" Queeg asked calmly, as he began to rock back and forth on his round body. "Quizzel, the great founder of the Galactic Association for Galaxy Guides and LX Travellers sought you out, decided you had what it takes to become a Guide and sent you to the Academy. Why did you go? Why did you train to become a Galaxy Guide?"

Fizz pondered Queeg's question for a moment. She didn't like being serious; she didn't like to think too hard about why she had joined the Galactic Galaxy Guide Academy. It had all been so long ago.

"I didn't like the Galactic Council wiping out planets," she said, distantly. "I mean – a single, solitary council deciding who gets to live and who gets to die. That's not right, is it?"

"Indeed it is not," Queeg agreed. "Sarkon and I were once advisors to the Galactic Council but, when they began their … planet-relocation programme, we went a different way and left the Council's work behind us. They relocated your home planet, I believe?"

Fizz fidgeted uncomfortably on the table, straightened her legs, crossed them again and looked across at Kevin, who was hovering nearby, listening to every word.

"The Council decided that a planet populated by beings who could … well, to put it bluntly, just catch fire and explode spontaneously was too dangerous to exist in the Galaxy," she said.

"Was that when Quizzel found you?" Queeg asked softly. "When TemperTantrumonious was relocated?"

Fizz nodded, not meeting Queeg's eyes.

"They never asked *us* what *we* thought could be done," she said, her eyes welling with tears. "I mean, the spontaneous combustion is a genetic trait, a part of our DNA. Most of us could control it; there were only a few mad TemperTantrumous who caused trouble."

"The Galactic Council just towed and relocated TemperTantrumonious?" Queeg said. "They never even tried to find a more … peaceful solution?"

Fizz shook her head.

"So you became a Galaxy Guide, so you could help other species, other civilisations, survive and live on after their planet had been relocated."

"Evacuees from a relocation planet could be sent to Squetania Blib to live," Fizz replied. "It's in uncharted space; the Galactic Council doesn't even know it's there. Right now there are over a hundred different species all living there, all evolving, surviving and starting again, and all of them living peacefully and harmoniously."

Queeg's legs extended again; he wobbled to his feet and shuffled over to Fizz.

"Sarkon and I want the same as you do, Galaxy Guide," he said. "We want to stop the Galactic Council wiping out entire species at will, just because they feel they are unworthy of existing in the Galaxy."

"But ... Earth was in breach of the Interstellar Bill of Law, wasn't it?" Fizz asked. "Humans weren't living peacefully with their co-habitants."

"The human race is a deeply flawed species and it has much to learn about tolerance and appreciation of its world and fellow inhabitants, that is true," Queeg said. "But humans will learn, the hard way, and eventually they will see the error of their ways and stop destroying their planet; stop mindlessly wiping out other species and themselves. Let's remember, one day Earth will be ruled by the worms and the human race will have to learn to change."

Fizz glanced curiously at Kevin and silently mouthed:

"Worms?"

"Indeed ..." Queeg said, smiling. "Worms. In the meantime, none of that changes the fact that the Galactic Council has gone too far this time. They have exterminated millions of species living on the Earth: species that have always lived peacefully and harmoniously with every other being. In the simplest of terms, the Galactic Council's decision to relocate the Earth was wrong ... terribly, terribly wrong. That wrong must be righted and the Earth given a second chance. The only way that can be done is by going back in time and preventing the Earth being relocated in the first place."

"And the Galaxy?" Fizz said.

"The Galaxy is in danger, unfortunately, because of the mistake you and Dawn Gray made when you DROSSed off the Earth the first time. As I explained before, the Earth is dead and yet a human being still exists somewhere in the Galaxy; that is very confusing for the Vortex. It will keep rerunning time and the Earth will keep getting relocated until the Vortex has sorted the disruption out – which, of course, it never will, so long as Earth ceases to exist and a human continues to live."

"So time repeating itself, the Earth getting towed over and over again, is a bit like an instant replay playing."

Queeg nodded.

"If looking at it like that helps you to understand … yes."

"And Mantor, when he found us, was trying to wipe Dawn out, erase her from time?"

"He was. That is what he does and what he still does."

"Still does?" Fizz said, the alarm and worry clear in her tone.

"Oh yes, Mantor lives," Queeg replied. "And he will begin his search for Dawn Gray imminently. He has been programmed to find her and destroy her, and he will not stop until that mission is complete."

"Great," Fizz said.

"Tewwific," Kevin added.

"What about those things I saw kill you on Earth?" Fizz suddenly remembered. "What were they all about? Where did they come from?"

"Do not concern yourself with them, Galaxy Guide," Queeg said, reassuringly. "They will not seek you out; they are looking only for me."

"Who are they?"

"Vortex Demons," Queeg replied. "Bounty hunters hired by the Galactic Council. Do not forget, Sarkon and I left the Council because of their planet-relocation programme, and the Galactic Council does not take kindly to interference when they are trying to find a rogue Earthling and remove her from time and space. Vortex Demons are … well, *what* they are is not important. The Demons are not something any creature needs to worry themselves about unless they absolutely have to. Trust me and just hope you are never unlucky enough to have one hired to hunt you down. Just take comfort in the fact that they will hunt only those whom they are told to hunt, and they have been instructed by the Galactic Council to hunt me and stop me from hindering their search for Dawn Gray."

Fizz looked at Queeg for a moment. There was a lot she suddenly felt she wanted to tell him, a lot she wanted him to know about just how much she was beginning to admire and like him – but she had the feeling that friends and admiration were not what interested a Superintendent and Regulator for the Space-Time Vortex.

"So I find Dawn," Fizz finally said.

"Yes," Queeg replied.

"We go back in time, back to when the Trygonian Recovery Vessel is about to tow the Earth."

"Yes."

"And … then what."

"Eggs," Queeg replied, somewhat cryptically.

"What?"

"TimeEggs," he said, pointing to the box on the table with the five transparent-looking eggs in it. "The most sought-after, treasured possession any being could ever own in this Galaxy. These are the only five in existence."

"What do they do?" Fizz asked.

"Come closer," Queeg replied, stretching out a thin, spindly arm and taking one of the eggs from the box, "and I'll show you."

18

the timeeggs

Queeg took one of the TimeEggs from the box as Fizz moved closer. Kevin hovered nearer, his pale blue eyes sparkling in wonder as Queeg took the egg, cracked its shell gently against the edge of the table and then threw it up into the air.

Time …

… can …

… stand …

… still …

It's that simple.

Nobody can truly understand time and nobody ever will.

Sixty seconds in a minute?

Sixty minutes in an hour?

Twenty-four hours in a day?

Seven days in a week?

Says who?

Timekeeping with clocks and such like was an idea thought up by human beings and, even before that, the process of telling the time by sunlight and with sundials ... all a human idea, a human innovation.

The truth is that time is everywhere, all around us, and for those beings who know how, and who have things like TimeEggs, it can be manipulated. Not controlled, understand that – time can never be *controlled*; but it can be adjusted and it can be broken into sections, pockets, dimensions.

As the TimeEgg hovered in the air, its two halves floating several feet apart, Fizz found herself standing and wondering just exactly what was supposed to be happening.

"That's lovely," she said, sarcastically. "A floating egg: wonderful. Did you invent that, or was it some Galactic genius who had too much free time on his hands?"

"Your sarcastic wit will be your undoing one day, Galaxy Guide," Queeg replied, somewhat scornfully. "Robot?" Kevin hovered closer to Queeg, his blue eyes slightly faded in nervous anticipation of why he had suddenly been called into the discussion. "I wonder if you'd be so kind as to help me with a demonstration."

"Demonstwation?" Kevin repeated. "What kind of demonstwation?"

"Yeah," Fizz added. "What kind of demonstwation? I mean, demonstration?"

"All I want you to do, my little robot friend, is fly between the two broken halves of the TimeEgg."

Kevin looked at the halves of the egg and the gap of thin air between them, which was just big enough for him to pass through.

"Fly between the two bwoken halves?"

"If you would," Queeg reassured with a smile.

Kevin flew slowly towards the gap between the two TimeEgg halves, pausing just an inch or so in front of it.

"What's going to happen to …?" He didn't have time to finish his sentence. Unexpectedly, Queeg reached out a thin arm and pushed Kevin the last few inches forward between the two halves of the TimeEgg.

Kevin vanished.

"Where'd he go?" Fizz asked, slightly concerned. "That's very disturbing, you know. Where did he go?"

"Who knows?" Queeg replied quite nonchalantly. "Into an artificial Time Pocket is my best guess."

"Explanation time, Queegy," Fizz said, putting her hands on her hips and fixing Queeg with a stern look. "I'm lost."

"The TimeEgg, or, as it is better known Trippycarius Ellipticae, is grown on the dark side of the planet Ellipticae Be¬x. The dark side of Ellipticae Be¬x just happens to be the closest point to The Crysta-Void, the biggest and deadliest black hole in the Galaxy. It is as a direct result of its geographical location, so close to the Crysta-Void, that the TimeEgg has such wondrous and mysterious qualities. Its geographical location also makes it difficult to get to the Trippycarius Ellipticae, which is why TimeEggs are so rare. Most people who try to reach the plant that bears these eggs end up getting sucked into the Crysta-Void and are never heard from again."

"And how exactly are these … Tryppi … Elipticary … TimeEggs supposed to help me and Dawn save the Earth and every being in the known Galaxy again?" Fizz asked, as she gazed at the shimmering, clear light that flickered between the halves of the TimeEgg.

"That … I do not know," Queeg replied, and with that he plucked the two halves of the TimeEgg from the air. Instantly, Kevin reappeared out of thin air.

"What?!" Fizz exclaimed, completely ignoring Kevin's sudden reappearance.

"Where am I?" Kevin muttered.

Queeg tossed the used and useless halves of the TimeEgg onto the table.

"What do you mean … you don't know?" Fizz bellowed again.

"Am I safe?" Kevin went on to himself. "Am I all wight? I don't wemember what just happened to me."

Queeg turned to Fizz calmly.

"I am giving you this gift, Galaxy Guide. The gift is the power to freeze time, to paralyse it, to halt it and to remove from time anything, or any*one*, you wish. In short … to create an artificial Time Pocket and hide in that Pocket anything you wish. How you and the Earth girl choose to use my gift only you can decide, when the time is right."

"I mean," Kevin went on, "One minute I was here, the next second evewything went weally weird."

"Shut up!" Fizz shouted at Kevin. "You're back now, aren't you? Safe and sound; eve*wy*thing's fine now, so just button it a second, will you?"

"Charming," Kevin mumbled.

"We decide?" Fizz continued to rant. "*We* decide? Oh, this just gets better and better! You're gonna send us back through time to save an entire planet, to save the entire Galaxy, and *we*'ve got to figure out how to do it!? No hints, no tips, no ideas? Just … jump in this tunnel and away you go; oh … by the way, don't forget your eggs!"

"Are you finished?" Queeg said calmly.

"Yes, I'm finished!" Fizz screamed. "But I'm not happy. So there."

"Good," Queeg replied, as he picked up the Time Tunnel from the table, pushed a series of buttons and tapped the handle on the table. Instantly, in a flash of light, a new Time Tunnel unravelled itself at a frightening speed, spiralling forward out of the door on the other side of the room and disappearing somewhere below them – somewhere in the reaches of space.

The whooshing sound began to come from the open end of the Time Tunnel just in front of Fizz, and she could feel it pulling her in.

"Just remember," Queeg said. "The TimeEgg cuts time off, freezes whatever comes between the two halves. It harnesses powers gained from exposure to the Crysta-Void; it is a temporary portal in time. Anything between the broken halves, anything caught in its field, is safe from anything and anyone."

Fizz looked at Queeg, wondering if he was trying to tell her what she was already thinking.

Queeg handed Fizz the Locator-Sphere and the little black box. She placed the Locator-Sphere in her hip bag and held the box in her hands.

"What is this?"

"It is your ship," Queeg replied, matter-of-factly. "It is a Holoship, transparent from the outside and completely weightless. From the inside, however, it is as solid, reliable and safe as any Trygonian Council Vessel. It can transport you to the point in time where you need to be, once you have found the Earth girl. It is fast, Galaxy Guide … very, very fast."

Fizz rolled the tiny black box around in the palm of her hand.

"My ship huh? Can't I just use an LX-Dome to get to where we need to be?"

"I think it is safe to say that your ability to use LX Domes safely and securely has been proven to be … questionable, wouldn't you say?" Queeg said. "Have faith, Galaxy Guide, the Holoship will work for you; trust me. I am giving you the TimeEggs … there are four left, but you will only need one. Nevertheless, take great care with them. If you could manage to save one or two when this is all over, I would appreciate it."

Fizz stuffed the holoship and the box of TimeEggs into her hip bag with the Locator-Sphere and secured it more tightly around her waist.

"How do I know I'm going to find Dawn at the end of this Time Tunnel?"

"You will find her," Queeg replied. "We have intercepted information sent to the Galactic Council by one of their own, a being who is also looking for Dawn Gray – Mantor."

Fizz and Kevin exchanged terrified glances.

"While you are wasting time making idle chitchat with me, he is making his way to Dawn Gray. It is time for you to go. You must reach her before Mantor does."

Fizz sat down at the mouth of the Time Tunnel, feeling the powerful air sucking her in and the whooshing from inside the tunnel streaming up all around her.

"This sucks," she whispered to herself.

"Um … you know what?" Kevin said, hovering close to Fizz's ear. "I weally don't like the look of this Time Tunnelly thingy. I don't think I'll twy it wight now. I mean, it's been a vewy twaumatic expewience, all this, you know? What with being stuck in a Time Pocket and all that so I think I'll just …"

Fizz wrapped her arm around Kevin's shiny, metallic body and let the Time Tunnel suck them both in.

In a millisecond, they were gone and Queeg was alone – or so he thought.

As he turned to leave, the Time Tunnel slowly closing behind him, he was suddenly faced with an enormous, towering creature. Queeg had never seen the being before and he had no idea how he had managed to get into the Eye of the Galaxy, but he knew instantly who it was. When a message ran across the bandage-covered computer screen, Queeg knew he was right.

SEE

UNDERSTAND

DECIDE

the message read.

Queeg saw, he understood and he decided.

Decided, there and then, that it was time for him to die … again.

19

the stars of the show

The cages hovering above the ground were led out of the Performers' Confinement Zone in single file. At the back of the line, Dawn and Dawn were carried along with Zak's solid cage just a short way in front of them.

As they emerged into the brightly lit arena, a thunderous cheer went up as thousands and thousands of Grakons settled in for the show.

The cages floated up, way above the cheering, jeering Grakons, until all of them were hovering high above the ground and moving around above the crowd.

The two Dawns squinted as the bright lights of the arena flashed and sparkled, but below them they could clearly see Orlak, in his top hat and long coat, taking centre stage in the arena. His over-long, creepily-thin legs moved graciously and methodically as he held his arms outstretched on either side of him and addressed the Grakon masses.

"NAK-TAA!" Orlak bellowed in his hissing growl. "NAK-TAA!" The Grakon crowd fell silent. "Welcome ... loyal Grakons to – Spectalica-*GALACTICA*!" The cheers went up again and many of the Grakons in the crowd jumped to their feet and began applauding wildly. Orlak silenced them all with a raised hand and an approving nod of his head.

"We have many wondrous sights and surprises for you to feast your eyes upon tonight! So ... let us wait no longer and bring out our first Galactic anomaly! Our first freak of space and time! Welcome, Grakons ... *friends*; welcome to the arena the Ryataar!" Dawn and Dawn watched in horror as the wild and uncontrollable Grakon crowd all jumped to their feet and began cheering and jeering again as a small, human-looking creature was dropped from his cage into the centre of the arena. Dawn had come across a Ryataar before. She had mistaken him for a human until she had seen the hundreds of little roots that sprouted from the lower half of his body.

The Ryataar in the centre of the arena was running around frantically, looking for somewhere to hide away from the jeering mob of Grakons that were in the process of throwing things at him and booing. The Ryataar looked exactly as any human would, but from the waist down he was nothing more than roots – the same as any tree would have.

It was his Life-Roots that were pulling him around the arena, clutching on to any surface they could find to pull him out of the line of savage abuse that was being hurled towards the centre of the arena. Orlak cackled and laughed manically as he chased the little Ryataar around the arena, cracking a flashing blue Holowhip at his first spectacle to keep him from running into cover in some dark corner somewhere.

The Holowhip snapped loudly and hissed as Orlak cracked it around the Ryataar and the poor creature just kept running, his face a permanent expression of sheer terror and anger as he was subjected to further humiliation.

"This is horrible," Dawn's alternative self said, dabbing at her teary eyes with the grubby woollen sleeve of her pyjamas. "That poor thing."

"Oh he's just the warm-up," Zak called out from a little way ahead of them. "It's gonna get much better than this."

"You enjoy this or something?" Dawn snapped. She still couldn't quite see Zak's face properly; his back was slightly turned and the bright lights of the arena, after the gloomy darkness of the Confinement Zone, had left Dawn with flashing spots in front of her eyes.

"Me? Oh yeah, I'm having a blast … aren't you?" At first, Dawn thought Zak was hunched down in his cage, chuckling to himself as he watched the little Ryataar getting chased around the arena by Orlak and his Holowhip, but as she looked closer she actually thought he was crying.

"Are you okay?"

"I'm fine," Zak spat in response. "My turn soon; you'll like my spot – everyone always loves me. Bit like you, see? The last of my kind, the only one like me left alive anywhere. Everyone loves to see the Zaktillianprototypicarus."

"The *what*?" Dawn said.

Slowly, Zak stood and turned around, wobbling in his hovering cage. For the first time, Dawn could see his face and she was stunned, amazed and slightly disturbed to see that he was an android. But, she had to admit, a rather good-looking android.

"You're …" she hesitated.

"An android," Zak interrupted. "I know."

"Actually," Dawn said, feeling her face flush and wondering, before she even said it, why exactly she said it, "I was going to say ... cute."

Zak looked a little bit like a patchwork doll. His hair, spiky and black and stiff, looked as though it had been stuck on with glue; his face looked as if it was made of cheap material and it was covered in black cotton that was stitched all around to hold his face together. Zak's eyes were wide and a deep brown colour, and they possessed the same forlorn expression that a naughty puppy has when it's done something... well, naughty.

"I'm Zaktillianprototypicarus, Zak for short," Zak went on, vacantly. "The first fully functional, made-to-order, first and last of its kind, Cross-matter AOS."

"AOS?" Dawn repeated.

"Artificial Off-spring," Zak explained.

"Artificial Off-spring?" Dawn repeated again.

"Cross-matter," Zak said. "That means I'm a cross between an organic living being and a machine. All the important things – brain, heart, lungs, stomach – everything a healthy living being needs to be ... well, to be real ... I've got. But everything else is super, hyper-efficient titanium alloy. Strong, resistant, durable and one hundred per cent fire-proof. I was the first and last AOS: a prototype child that was going to be available for adoption for any couple in the Galaxy who couldn't have children of their own and who could afford me. I could love, think, eat, breathe – everything a wanna-be parent would want in a child, with the added bonus that I was solid and functional and could help perform daily, household tasks, from fixing a leaky tap to single-handedly changing the wheel on a car. I was gonna be in demand. I was supposed to be a success. I was supposed to be perfect."

Far below, the Grakons were on their feet and cheering again as a Glumph, a rare and somewhat simple giant life-form, was paraded around before them on a big metal lead and made to demonstrate his immense strength by lifting up entire benches of laughing, cheering Terra Firmakon Grakons. The other Dawn was sobbing desperately as she watched the poor, confused Glumph being booed and hissed at, but not knowing why.

Dawn huddled closer to the bars of the cage and held a hand out to Zak. She wanted to be there for him and hold his ... well, his kind of weird, metallic-webbed hand. She wanted to comfort him any way she could; he looked so lonely all of a sudden, so lost.

"What happened?" she whispered.

Zak slid down the bars of his cage and collapsed in a heap on the floor.

"They couldn't get the skin right," he said, as if he were talking about not being able to perfect a recipe for peppermint creams. "It's hard to replicate human skin, you know. It's soft and smooth, but amazingly tough and durable too. I was given this." Zak touched his own cloth-like complexion and Dawn tried to stretch through her bars to touch it, but Zak's cage was floating too far away.

"The best they could come up with was this Klyonian cloth, stitched together with black thread. Ridiculous, isn't it? They can build a living, breathing life-form that's twice as strong, twice as fast and twice as smart as almost any other being, but they couldn't replicate skin. Makes you laugh, doesn't it?"

Zak smiled to himself, but Dawn had to admit that she didn't think it made her want to laugh one little bit.

"Needless to say," Zak went on, "when they put me out there in the public eye and tried to sell me, tried to get funding to make more like me, everyone freaked out – said I was some kind of sick half-breed, that I didn't know what I was and that I shouldn't be allowed to exist at all, let alone be allowed to enter a family's home. They scrapped the Cross-matter AOS Programme after that and threw me on the rubbish heap. That was when Orlak found me."

Below, Orlak was about to announce the next act into the arena, but Dawn suddenly noticed that the Grakons' hysterical cheering had quietened slightly, and there was now a feeling of unease and frustration in the air.

"Why's it gone so quiet?" Dawn asked, in a hushed voice.

"I don't know," Zak replied, peering through his bars and down into the arena.

"Where are the Earthlings?" one of the Grakons bellowed out from the crowd.

"You promised Earthlings!" another voice called out.

"All in good time, my Grakon friends!" Orlak announced, trying to calm the increasing hostility. "At Spectalica-Galactica, we save the best till last! Let me show you now … our Zaktillianprototypicarus! The only Cross-matter AOS in existence!"

"Seen him!" a particularly gruesome-looking Grakon screamed, interrupting Orlak's flow. "We've all seen that little freak before! We want the Earthlings!"

Even from their position, hovering high above the arena, the two Dawns and Zak could see Orlak growing more and more nervous. He stumbled around the arena, his spindly legs almost becoming entangled as he tried to hush the angry mob of Grakons.

"Looks like you two have just earned me the night off," Zak said, with a sympathetic smile.

"*We want the Earthlings. We want the Earthlings. We want the Earthlings. We want the Earthlings. We want the Earthlings!*"

The Grakons' chant grew louder and angrier until, eventually, Orlak raised a long, bony, black hand and signalled for Dawn and Dawn's cage to be opened.

"It'll be over quickly," Zak said comfortingly, as he stretched out his arm through his bars. Dawn pushed her hand out and, for the briefest of seconds, their fingertips touched. As they did, the bottom fell out of the two Dawns' cage and the pair found themselves, suddenly, flat on their backs and in the centre of the arena.

They expected booing.

They expected hissing and jeering. They expected to look up and see thousands of wild, angry, leering Grakons bearing down on them.

Instead, however, as the two Dawn Grays sat themselves up and looked around, all they saw were stunned faces, and all they heard from the thousands of enormous Grakons was complete and total silence.

20

the galactic council adjourns

"Useless, the lot of them!" Empress Garcea fumed, as she literally flew along the bright hallways of the Galactic Council's headquarters. Jevkaa Creebo was hurrying to keep up, the fixed expression of sympathy and understanding on his Liquisage rippling beneath its clear mask as he ran.

It was uncommon for a Luminious life-form to express a feeling of rage or anger, but when they did it was quite a sight to witness. Empress Garcea hovered higher and higher above the floor as she flew along, and the calm, shimmering light that emitted from her body was now trembling and burning a brighter, darker orange colour. Her six pale eyes were darkening too – to a deep, almost purple colour.

"I announce that Mantor has survived, that he has escaped the Time Pocket and that he is in pursuit of the Earth girl again – and what does the Council say? Nothing! How do they react when I tell them that the despicable, hateful planet Earth will soon be wiped from history forever? They don't! Not one of them so much as batted an eyelid."

"Empress," Jevkaa interrupted, politely and submissively. "I think, if I may be so bold, the reason your fellow members of the Galactic Council ... struggle to react or show interest in your news and your announcements is that ..."

Empress Garcea slowed to a halt and spun gracefully around to face Jevkaa.

"That what, Jevkaa? That what?"

"Well ..." Jevkaa bowed his head submissively again. "That they're all dead," he said. "They've all been dead for many aeons now, Empress, since you killed them all when you first came to power as Head of the Galactic Council."

The Empress studied Jevkaa for a moment. The expression on his Liquisage was now apologetic and remorseful.

"Hmm," Empress Garcea said, floating down to the ground to be closer to Jevkaa. "I think you make an excellent point, my faithful Jevkaa," she said, honestly. "Once again I thank you for showing me direction and calming me in a moment of anger and frustration."

Jevkaa's Liquisage bubbled and melted and set itself again, this time in an expression of happiness and love.

It was true. Jevkaa's explanation of why the Galactic Council were so unanimated was completely accurate, as hard as that might be to understand or even believe. The Galactic Council, the governing body in complete and total control of the entire Galaxy and the Space-Time Vortex itself, consisted of one member: Empress Garcea of Grahl.

She had murdered the other Council members by poisoning them on the very first day she was allowed to take her seat in office. Because Grahlanians such as Empress Garcea were considered for so long to be a sub-species by the rest of the Galaxy, none moreso than the members of the Galactic Council, when she was finally allowed to take her seat on the Council she was filled with a need for revenge – and she took that revenge immediately and without mercy.

Empress Garcea was able to poison five of the seven Council members and, perhaps for sentimental reasons, she choose to keep the dead, rotting remains of these members sitting around the huge table in the Council Assembly Room on Everesta 9. The only two Council members she was unable to murder were Sarkon Gartillius and Queeg. They had not been at the Council's headquarters when the Empress set about taking her revenge and, upon learning what had happened and of the plans Empress Garcea had in store for the Galaxy, they never returned. It was these two rogue, ex-Council members that Empress Garcea was most interested in now.

"What of Queeg and Sarkon?" she asked Jevkaa, as she began gliding, much more elegantly and calmly now, along the corridors.

"There has been word from Mantor himself," Jevkaa replied, scurrying along behind. "He reports that Queeg has been …" – Jevkaa cleared his throat – "finished, although I suspect the Vortex Demons will continue their pursuit, just to make sure. You know how difficult it can be to get rid of Queeg, Highness. Sarkon, obviously, is a little more difficult to locate."

"Of course he is," the Empress said, smiling. "A being that holds no physical shape or presence and that can mould and melt itself into anything is always going to be tricky to find; but have faith, Jevkaa … Have faith in my Mantor, in my boy. I do."

"Of course, Highness," Jevkaa bowed. "Mantor will succeed in carrying out your wishes, of that I have no doubt."

"And the Earth girl?" Empress Garcea went on. "Dawn Gray? Has he located her?"

"He is following two beings, the TemperTantrumous and the robot, along a Time Tunnel he believes will lead him to the Earth girl."

"Then we leave immediately, Jevkaa." Empress Garcea glided away from Jevkaa, who began following. "I want to be with my Mantor when he finds Dawn Gray. I want to witness the end of the Earth, the end of its memory, of its history, of its very existence."

"As you please, Highness," Jevkaa said, now struggling to keep up with a frantic and excitable Empress. "I believe Mantor began his pursuit from a Time Tunnel located in The Eye of the Galaxy."

"Good," the Empress said, smiling. "Then to The Eye of the Galaxy we shall go, Jevkaa. On the way I will locate Sarkon myself. We have some unfinished business together. Today the great Sarkon Gartillius will meet the same fate as Dawn Gray and the Earth."

21

spectalica-galactica's mystery stars

Slowly, Dawn and Dawn got to their feet. Nobody made a sound and nobody moved. The two girls held hands tightly and peered around at the sea of scaly, glassy-eyed creatures that were staring at them in amazement.

From behind the two Dawns, Orlak began creeping his way around, his long, thin legs not making a sound as he observed a sight the likes of which he had never seen before.

All in all the Grakons were a rather wild, savage species, who were not used to socialising or entertaining, and had all the manners of a starved Triple-headed Raktaar Monkey with bad breath and a foul temper. They should have been on the Earth girls in a flash. They should have been jeering and hooing and shoving them around and pulling them about, trying to get a closer look.

In fact, Orlak had half-expected the need for extra security measures to protect his two new prize attractions. He thought, that once they actually saw them, the Grakons would really be after blood.

But it was quite the opposite.

A few of the Grakons were actually climbing down from their seats and were walking across the arena towards the Earthlings. More Grakons followed, and before long the entire Grakon audience was standing in the arena and staring with wide, black, glassy eyes at Dawn Gray and her alternative self.

"What-are-they-doing?" the other Dawn whispered, out of the corner of her mouth.

"I-have-no-idea," Dawn replied, squeezing her name-sake's hand tighter and trying hard not to meet any of the Grakons' eyes.

The Grakons continued to slither and squelch around the arena for some minutes. Their flippers flapped and their gills hissed and puffed as they breathed in the moist Grakonian air. They made funny sort of grunting noises as a few of them poked and prodded the two Dawns, not in a particularly threatening way but rather in a kind of respectful awe.

Then, as if things were not confusing and slightly worrying enough, above the arena came an enormous cracking sound and, high above them there was a flash of light, followed by something shiny, silver and hard falling at a wonderfully insane speed towards the ground.

The two Dawns took cover, as did Orlak and most of the Grakons. However, one Grakon in particular did not take cover; instead, he simply stayed rooted to the spot and watched with a kind of dumb fascination as the shiny silver thing got faster and closer and closer and faster until …

… it hit him squarely on the head, killing him instantly.

The Grakon collapsed to the floor amidst a flurry of terrified and angry bellows from its fellows. The shiny silver object hit the dusty floor of the arena with a tinny-sounding thud, rolled around a bit and then, in a split second, hovered up into the air. It seemed to find its bearings and opened up two little flaps to reveal the palest, calmest, prettiest eyes Dawn had ever seen.

She had, of course, seen them before.

"Oh, I am so sowwy," the little robot apologised. "Am I intewwupting something?"

The mass of angry Grakons moved closer to the little robot, their faces filled with rage.

"Oh dear," the robot said. "I think I've awwived at the wong stop. I'm looking for a Dawn Gway … have any of you nice … cweatures seen her?"

"Kevin!" Dawn suddenly screamed. Kevin spun around and his wide eyes grew bluer. "Kevin?" Dawn said again. "What happened to you? Is that … a tail? Are those … ears?"

"Dawn Gway!" he called. And as he did, another larger, not quite so shiny object fell into the arena, with a discernably louder thud.

Fizz didn't hit any Grakons on her way into the arena, which was a bit of a shame really, because if she had she would have known what she was dealing with. As it was, Fizz got to her feet with her back to the mass of Grakons, facing Dawn and Dawn. She was, therefore, completely oblivious to the terrifyingly dangerous situation into which she had just arrived.

"Fizz?" Dawn said.

"Fizz?" the other Dawn said.

"Do I know you?" Fizz said, looking at Dawn's other self.

"I'm Dawn Gray – *another* Dawn Gray, I mean. We met in an alternative dimension." The alternative Dawn Gray held her hand out to Fizz; Fizz, in return, rolled her eyes and sighed exasperatedly.

"Two Dawn Grays: I mean who could ask for any more, who could want any more? I mean … this is just like a dream come true for me! Hooray, what a wonderful result … two Dawn Grays." Fizz lowered her voice and looked straight at Dawn, *her* Dawn, the Dawn she knew.

"All right, Dawn?" she said.

"All right, Fizz?" Dawn replied. "Missed ya."

Fizz smiled.

"You know what? Much as I hate to admit it, I've kinda missed you too, mate."

Dawn returned the smile as Fizz took her arm and took control of the situation.

"I'm here to find you and get you out of here, wherever exactly *here* is and … well, there's more, a lot more. I'll tell you on the way. Come on."

Fizz spun on her heels and crunched straight into an eight-foot Grakon.

The slimy, scaly Grakon peered down at her with his cold, black eyes, his gills flapping furiously as he huffed and puffed at the new intruder on his planet. He was truly a terrifying sight.

"'Scuse me, fish-face," Fizz said, actually rather politely. "Can I just squeeze past?"

Dawn covered her eyes; Fizz's lack of subtlety and decorum in sensitive situations never ceased to amaze her.

Kevin's shutters zipped down and, high above them, Zak roared with laughter.

Fizz turned back to Dawn.

"Do you know you're still wearing your pyjamas?"

"Yes, I know that, Fizz," Dawn said, bluntly. "Since we last saw each other, since you dumped me on a planet with only variants of myself for company, I haven't really had a chance to change, you know?"

"I'm still in my pyjamas too," the other Dawn threw into the conversation.

"They're pyjamas?" Fizz replied. "I thought something died on you." She turned back to the Grakon. "You gonna move? I have to be somewhere, you know? Worlds to save, Galactic destruction to avert and all that."

"Galactic destruction!?" Dawn repeated. "Again? I thought we sorted that out." Fizz slowly turned back to Dawn.

"Now, why would you think that? Me and you just *that* lucky, are we?"

Fizz turned back to the Grakon, who still had not moved.

"What's this guy's problem?" she said.

"The problem is ..." – a hissing tone came from behind Fizz – "that you've interrupted the show. I don't think this Grakon is happy." Fizz saw the spider-like creature, dressed in the long coat and top hat, creeping along towards her.

"Orlak?" she said.

"Who's Orlak?" Kevin said, peeping out from under one eye-shutter.

Fizz turned to Dawn.

"Are you …?" she said. Dawn nodded. "Is this …?" Both Dawns nodded. "You're stars in Spectalica-Galactica?" Fizz finally managed to say.

Dawn nodded again.

"That is so cool!" Fizz screamed excitedly. "I love this show!"

Just then, a cage dropped from high above them.

Zak tried to scream a warning, but he was too late. The glowing bars of the cage trapped Fizz and Kevin inside.

"I'm glad you like our show," Orlak said softly, as he crept in front of Fizz's cage. "Because you and your little robot friend have just become our latest attractions."

Now, what happened next could have been a good thing or a very, very bad thing, depending on how you wish to look at it. In the end, however, it turned out to be nothing but another strange and surprising twist in Dawn and Fizz's bizarrely-twisting fate.

Mantor arrived in the arena.

Need I say more?

The Time Tunnel had not yet finished depositing its travellers, and when he arrived there was another stunned silence across the entire arena – with the exception of Dawn, Fizz and Kevin, who managed to mutter similar phrases along the lines of:

"But … what … why … how …?"

Instantly Mantor spun around and faced Dawn. He stretched out an arm, clad in flesh-like armour plating, and in his steel-clawed hand a ball of electric-red light began to hiss and blaze.

Dawn was frozen to the spot with terror. Fizz tried to ram her way out of her cage, but to no avail.

"No!" she screamed. "Wait! Stop him! Someone, help her!"

But no one helped. No one moved.

The ball of deadly laser fire blazed in Mantor's hand and he stepped closer to Dawn, who still could not move.

SPACE-TIME MANIPULATOR LOCATED

the message ran on the monitor embedded in Mantor's skull. It was still slightly covered by the bandages he wore around his head to help disguise his bizarre appearance, but there was no mistaking the message; nor the one that followed:

TERMINATION IMMINENT

Finally Dawn found her senses coming to life, but all she could do was scream.

And then ... as Mantor raised his clawed hand and aimed the laser ball directly at her, his other arm wobbled like a jelly, changed colour briefly and then returned to its normal shape and length.

Everyone watched curiously as Mantor slowly turned his enormous skull and observed his arm.

As he did, the other arm did the same thing. It changed colour: bright blue this time. The laser ball in his hand disappeared and then the arm returned to its normal state.

Mantor seemed, all of a sudden, a bit confused. He lifted his head and looked back at Dawn.

I AM MANTOR

a new message ran, and immediately after that Mantor let out what could only really be described as a rather unpleasant belch. His head wobbled and changed shape slightly and, for a brief second, Dawn actually thought she saw a face on the monitor, but it was gone instantly.

I AM MANTOR

the message ran again, but by now no one was really sure what he was or what was going on.

I AM MANTOR

I AM MANTOR

I AM MANTOR

The message ran over and over again for a few seconds before Mantor squeaked, groaned, creaked, clicked and then … just flopped forward and was perfectly still, his monitor blank and messageless.

Fizz laughed out loud.

"That's so cool!" she cried. "He's broken!"

Another cage dropped down from above, this time enclosing Mantor inside. A third cage fell, and the two Dawns found themselves captive once again.

Orlak cracked his Holowhip at the Grakon masses and a thick cloud of smoke blew up in front of them.

"Take them away!" Orlak bellowed, and immediately the cages containing Fizz and Kevin, Dawn and Dawn and Mantor rose into the air and began hovering away from the arena and back to the Performers' Confinement Zone.

"What a show we have now!" Orlak cried gleefully, as his new prisoners were taken away. "What a show *I* have now!"

As the cages drifted through the smokescreen blocking the Grakons' view of what was happening, Dawn looked around her, not for her alternative self, not for Fizz and not even to see if Mantor was waking; she was looking for Zak.

Through the smoke she felt a cold, metallic hand touch her at the base of her spine. Dawn spun round and saw that Zak had extended his arm and penetrated the bars of her cage to reach her, just to touch her and reassure her.

Dawn smiled and squeezed Zak's artificial hand for comfort.

Zak smiled back.

"Don't worry," he mouthed at her, silently. "I'll look after you, whatever happens. I promise."

What was going to happen, however, nobody could have predicted. If Zak had known, he would not have made that promise, for it was a promise he would not be able to keep.

22

sarkon's demise?

Sarkon emerged from the swirling mass of cloud, with Queeg by his side, the pair of them ready to welcome their unwanted guests.

"Queeg," Empress Garcea said, softly and tunefully. "My old Superintendent. I thought you were dead."

"A pleasure to see you again, your highness," Queeg bowed slightly as the Empress approached him. "Regarding my death, I am eternal within the Space-Time Vortex, you remember?"

"Of course I do," Empress Garcea replied, smiling. "And you remember Jevkaa Creebo, my faithful aide." Queeg bowed at Jevkaa who, in response, changed the appearance on his Liquisage to one of humble greeting.

Empress Garcea looked up at the giant face of Sarkon Gartillius, swirling and shifting within the foggy cloud.

"You have no right being here, Empress," Sarkon said, in his deep, rumbling tone. "The Eye of the Galaxy is my domain. Nobody knows I am here." The Empress smiled.

"I know you're here, Sarkon."

Queeg's little arms and legs clicked back into his body, followed by his head, and he rolled himself across the ground between Sarkon and Empress Garcea.

His arms, legs and head reappeared and he stood, wobbly but determined. The Empress smiled again.

"Ever the faithful guardian, hmm, Queeg? Are you expecting trouble from me, Superintendent?"

"I expect nothing," Queeg replied. "And therefore I am never disappointed. Nor am I ever caught off guard."

Jevkaa shuffled forward and took his place between Queeg and his mistress, his Liquisage now showing a face which was as grimly determined as Queeg's stance indicated.

"Thank you, Jevkaa," Empress Garcea said quietly. "I have things under control. Do not alarm yourself." The Empress floated several more inches off the ground so she could meet Sarkon's enormous, misty eyes.

"You know why I am here," she said, clearly. "This really needn't become a destructive matter, Sarkon. The Galaxy is in dire trouble and life-forms … billions and billions of life-forms are in danger. The matter can be resolved, however, with the termination of a single Earthling."

Silence followed. Sarkon's clear, round eyes narrowed slightly and the mist around him darkened.

"An Earthling, Sarkon." the Empress repeated. "One little Earthling. Would the Galaxy really miss one … little … Earthling?"

"I cannot and will not speak for the beings of this Galaxy," Sarkon replied. "Nor will I comment on their thoughts and opinions."

"Diplomatic as ever," Empress Garcea chuckled.

"I could not say for sure whether the Galaxy would miss one little Earthling. I assume not – no more than most of us would miss one power-hungry, psychotic Luminious Empress."

Empress Garcea suddenly flashed a rather unnerving red colour and her calm and relaxed expression was replaced by one of anger and hatred.

"But I will say that the Galaxy will miss an entire planet," Sarkon went on. "It will miss an entire civilisation. And it will miss millions of species."

Empress Garcea floated higher, closer to Sarkon and Queeg suddenly stiffened, preparing for trouble.

"It was the Earth, Sarkon," the Empress said, softly. "Human beings were the plague of this Galaxy for aeons. Their waste, their pollution, their aggressive, murderous reputation spread through our Galaxy like a cancer. It had to be eliminated."

"You speak of humans, Empress," Sarkon said. "Human beings only. The Earth was populated by more than just human beings."

"It had to be done," the Empress said, flatly.

"Innocent life forms," Sarkon went on.

"It was a curse."

"These beings deserve life," Sarkon continued, ignoring the Empress.

"I did what I had to as head of the Galactic Council."

"The human race would have learned the error of their ways eventually. It would have been the hard way of doing things, but they would have learned."

"The Earth had to be relocated," Empress Garcea said determinedly.

"We are not to judge who becomes extinct and who does not."

"The Earth *had* to be relocated."

"It must be restored; the Vortex must be set straight and Earth must be allowed to thrive again and decide its own destiny."

"THE EARTH *HAD* TO BE RELOCATED!"

"YOU HAD NO RIGHT!" Sarkon suddenly exploded in a fit of rage, and with his outburst a thunderous clap of noise and bolts of electricity came flashing from the cloud and mist around him.

Empress Garcea remained calm.

Queeg and Jevkaa, still facing each other, trembled.

"Where is the Earth girl, Dawn Gray?" Empress Garcea said, calmly.

"Helping us," Sarkon replied. "Helping us to undo your evil."

"Where is she?" the Empress asked again, her luminous glow changing to red once again. She hovered so close to Sarkon now that she was almost floating between his enormous eyes.

"You cannot stop what we have begun, Empress." Sarkon's misty expression now seemed to be grinning. "If we go back in time and prevent the Earth being towed away in the first place, then the Trygonians will never return to Earth and your plans to relocate the planet will have been foiled. Earth will remain as it always has done – untouched, and none the wiser about how close it came to destruction.

And if you try to relocate it again, you would fail, because from now on … I will be watching you."

"Where is Dawn Gray?" Empress Garcea said again.

"Doesn't your despicable creation know?" Sarkon said, almost in a mocking kind of tone. "I thought Mantor, the great Space-Time Vortex manipulator, had found her. I thought that he was, at this very moment, terminating her and thus wiping Earth from the very memory of the Galaxy!"

Empress Garcea eyed Sarkon suspiciously.

"I grow tired of asking this Sarkon, so it will be for the last time. Where *is* the Earth girl?"

"No word from Mantor, Empress?" Sarkon continued to mock. "Oh dear, I do hope he hasn't met with foul play?"

Suddenly and without warning Empress Garcea flew, like a bolt of lightning, down towards Queeg. The Empress was nothing more than a single ball of energy as she engulfed the round robot and lifted him into the air.

"You cannot destroy Queeg, Empress," Sarkon bellowed. There was a hint of concern in his tone now.

The Empress's flaming stream of light flew towards the infinity of space which spread out before Sarkon. At the edge of space itself the Empress stopped and regained her natural form. She stood vast and towering, with Queeg rolled in a kind of blanket of burning red light that hung from her arm. She glared at Sarkon.

"I cannot destroy him, Sarkon," she sneered. "But I can lose him in the depths of space and time and leave him reeling and spinning through dimension after dimension for all eternity."

From the depths of space below where the Empress stood, shadows climbed. These shadows let out a terrifying, screeching wail as they shot up from the depths of space and began swirling around in front of the Empress.

Sarkon eyed the Empress curiously, as Queeg muttered from beneath the light which held him.

"No, Sarkon," he mumbled. "Tell her nothing."

"Dawn Gray is on Squetania Blib," Sarkon said in a low voice.

"LIAR!" Empress Garcea screamed, and with that the blanket of light streaming from her luminous body unravelled. Queeg was tossed out into the infinity of space like an old tin can.

As Queeg fell, the dark, ominous shadows shot through space and twisted around his plummeting body. Queeg was tossed and spun around, flashes of electric light illuminating his poor, helpless metal body as the shadows' piercing wails and screams floated up from the bottom of the Galaxy until, after just a few seconds, they were gone.

Queeg disappearing with them.

"NOOOO!" Sarkon bellowed, as Queeg's desperate calls for help rang out across the Galaxy.

"WHERE IS SHE!?" Empress Garcea screeched.

The cloud and mist of Sarkon's face thundered and swirled madly as the cloud darkened. The mist billowed forward towards the Empress, who flew at Sarkon, her arms outstretched, her colour blazing red, blue and purple.

The two collided, the cloud and the burning light, and there was a flash of brilliant, white light and a crash of deafening thunder.

Jevkaa watched in stunned amazement as the most astonishing lightning and thunderstorm began over his head.

The Eye of the Galaxy itself began to tremble. Jevkaa could have run, he could have found cover; he could have found a way out of the Eye.

But he did not.

He stood and watched as a one-on-one war between Empress Garcea and Sarkon Gartillius erupted over him.

Beneath Jevkaa's feet and all around him, the Eye of the Galaxy began to tremble and shake.

23

timeeggs and holoships

The Performers' Confinement Zone was as dark and gloomy as usual, and now more overcrowded than ever before. Despite this, however, Dawn took a little comfort and even a little bit of smug satisfaction in actually being the one familiar with their bizarre surroundings for a change, while Fizz looked slightly at a loss as to where she was or what she was going to do next.

"This is nice," Fizz said softly through the darkness. "Cosy, really homely. I love what you've done with the place."

Just a few feet away, beside the cage that held Fizz and Kevin, Dawn and Dawn's cage sat facing Zak, who was still held behind his own solid bars.

"I don't think you've got any right to be sitting there being funny, do you?" Zak said. "Everything was fine until you and that stupid little robot turned up."

"Stupid little wobot?" Kevin repeated. "I wesent that. You can't talk to me like that!"

"You tell him, Kev," Fizz said, getting to her feet and pressing her face as close to the glowing bars as she could.

"Just shut it, stitch face. Who did the sewing job on your mush anyway?"

"Watch it!" Zak snapped, now getting to his feet too. "Or you and your metal egg with ears are gonna find yourselves in a lot of trouble."

"Egg?" Kevin repeated again. "I weally don't think anyone could say I look like an egg."

"Eggs!" Fizz suddenly screamed, as she started foraging through her hip bag. She produced the little carton that contained the TimeEggs and opened it.

"What's that?" Dawn and Dawn said at the same time.

"Oh poo," Fizz said. She held up the egg box and showed Kevin the contents; two of the TimeEggs had been broken. Between the broken shells was nothing, just an empty space where the rest of the contents of the carton should have been.

"Well, you're just iwwesponsible, aren't you?" Kevin scoffed. "Two of those little eggy things broken already, and we've only been gone a short while."

"Yeah, yeah," Fizz said, lifting the broken shells out. Instantly, the rest of the carton and the remaining two TimeEggs reappeared. Fizz tossed the broken TimeEgg shells onto the ground. "Don't sweat, Kev. Still got two left."

Suddenly, the gloominess of the Confinement Zone was broken and a clear shaft of light appeared. In the beam, however, a very disturbing shadow loomed. The enormous cage floated into the room and set itself down on the ground beside Fizz and Kevin's cage. Inside the cage, Mantor wobbled precariously on his heavy metal heels. He was frozen, like a statue, his clawed hand still clasped as if the ball of laser fire were still clutched in his palm. Mantor rocked back and forth for a moment and then became perfectly still, his blank monitor, draped with torn, tatty bandages, looking directly over Fizz.

"I don't like the new neighbours," Fizz joked in a trembling voice. "I think it's time to move. Anyone know a way out of here?"

Dawn and Dawn turned to Zak.

"I can get us out," he said. "But I'm not helping you."

"Oh, really?" Fizz snapped. "Well, that's cool, Stitch. I've been in worse scrapes than this without you around before now. I'm sure I can figure something out, so don't you trouble yourself, okay?"

Slowly, Dawn reached her hand out through her bars. Seeing this, Zak extended his own arm and allowed Dawn to place her hand in his metallic, webbed palm. Dawn smiled at him. Her heart was racing but she wasn't really sure why. There was – something about Zak, something about the way he was, something about … *him* that just made her want to be close to him, to help him and to involve him in everything she did.

"Help us," Dawn whispered. "Please. Help us to get out of here and you can come with us."

"*Us?*" Zak said, softly.

"Me," Dawn replied, not really knowing why. "I want you to come with *me*."

Zak stared at Dawn. She was lovely and he liked looking at her, but even more than that, he liked her looking at him. Usually most beings he had come across in the Galaxy found it difficult to look at him; they only saw the bizarre mistake that, deep down, Zak knew he was. But Dawn Gray didn't. Dawn looked at him with … well, to be honest, he didn't really know how to describe the way she looked at him. But he knew he liked it and he knew that the more she looked at him, the more he wanted to do anything he could to be with her, help her and protect her.

"I can get us out!" Zak suddenly shouted. Dawn's heart lifted and a smile spread across her face as she gazed proudly at Zak. "I can get us out of these cages. I can get us out of Spectalica-Galactica – if you're all quick and you all do exactly as I say. After that, though, here on Grakonia … I can't do much without some sort of transport.

Everyone turned to Fizz, who was standing tall and proud in her cage and throwing something small and black up and down in her hand. It was the Holoship.

"I'll do you a deal, Stitch," she said with a wink. "You get me out of this flea-infested cesspool, and I'll do the rest … 'kay?"

24

the friends catch up

They all agreed to wait until later that night, when everything was still and quiet, to attempt their escape. As the night drew on, one by one the other caged beings and creatures all around them in the Confinement Zone began to snore, mumble and grumble in their sleep. Kevin slipped his shutters down and hovered close to the ground. Zak rested his eyes as he leant back against the solid bars of his cage – bars, he hoped, he would soon see the back of for good. The other Dawn Gray wrapped her arms around herself; still dressed in her filthy, woollen pyjamas she looked like a little lost orphan living on the street as she slumped down sideways and eventually ended up in a snoring heap on the floor.

"So what's *her* story?" Fizz asked, quietly. She was sitting in her cage as close to Dawn as she could get. The pair of them hugged their legs close to their bodies and rested their chins on their knees.

"She's me," Dawn replied, flatly. Fizz looked at her quizzically.

"She's … you? As in … *you* you? Like, Dawn Gray you?" Dawn simply nodded.

"Freaky," Fizz said. "Where'd you get her? Can you get a refund if you take her back?"

"On the planet you sent me to when we DROSSed off Earth the second time."

Fizz smiled, embarrassed. "Yeah, sorry about that. Don't know what happened there. If it's any consolation, I haven't had a much better time myself. What with Queeg and Sarkon and giant squirrels and Time Tunnels ... your parents freaking me out ... eggs ... Squigs ... this place."

"Whoa, whoa!" Dawn interrupted, holding up her hands. "What do you mean, my parents freaking you out? Where are my mum and dad this time, Fizz?"

"Last time I saw," Fizz replied, "they were frozen in time and quite safe. Queeg did it; not sure how, to be honest – must have used a really big TimeEgg, I s'pose."

"I don't care about Queeg!" Dawn blurted out. Her outburst was loud enough to cause the other Dawn and a few other dozing bodies in the darkness to stir and grumble a little louder. "I don't care about Queeg," Dawn repeated in a whisper. "Whoever he is. What about my parents ... why did they freak you out?"

"Well ... seems something went wrong with the DROSS: the second time we did it, I mean. You ended up on the planet where you found *her*," Fizz nodded her head at the sleeping Dawn Gray. "I ended up right back where I started, with the Trygonian Council Recovery Vessel floating overhead and your neighbours running around in a panic."

"And?" Dawn said impatiently. "Go on ... where were my mum and dad?"

"Right where they should have been: sitting on your front lawn, dressed for light-speed travel, in their swimming hats and sunglasses, wearing their earmuffs and covered in sunblock. Only problem was …" Fizz trailed off as she searched her mind for the best way to put it.

"Yeah? The only problem was what?"

"Was that they didn't have a clue who you were," Fizz said.

"What?" Dawn snapped. Again, several disgruntled voices grumbled and grunted through the darkness. "How could they not know who *I* am?" Dawn said, a little more quietly. "You mean they, like, *forgot* about me?"

"Not exactly," Fizz replied.

"They had amnesia or something?"

"No, their marbles were all there as far as I could tell."

"Well, what then? How could they not know who I was?"

"It was just the simple case that … well, in that dimension, whatever dimension it was I had landed myself in, whatever alternative Earth I was standing on … you didn't exist. In that time, Mr and Mrs Gray didn't have any children."

For a moment Dawn couldn't speak. She didn't know what to say, didn't know even where to begin. Finally she managed to mutter:

"They're okay though, right?"

"What does it matter?" Fizz replied, a little unsympathetically. "They're not *your* mum and dad. They're not from your time, not from your dimension. If anything happened to them, it wouldn't affect you or your real parents."

"That is a cold and horrible way of looking at it, Fizz," Dawn said. "Do you even have a clue what's happened to *my* parents?"

"Well, if time serves right, and the Galaxy is infinite and keeps repeating itself until the Space-Time Vortex straightens itself out … they're probably doing the same thing they were doing before. Probably back on that planet as king and queen of that weird little world. Time's in a rut here, Dawn. Things are just going over and over, backwards and forwards, until it sorts itself out." Fizz paused and took a deep breath. "That's kind of why I came looking for you again," she said.

Dawn looked across at her old friend and saw something in Fizz's face – a knowing yet wary glint of mischief in her eyes that made Dawn feel extremely nervous and a little bit scared.

25

fizz's bombshell

She didn't say anything, of course. Dawn knew that Fizz was simply pausing for dramatic effect, and soon enough she would blurt out the horrible, terrifying facts that were sure to rock Dawn's world even more.

Dawn had to wait about three and a half seconds.

"ThethingistheGalaxyisstillcollapsingandtheonlyonesthatcansaveitareusandwehavetogobackintimeandchangethingsanditsverydangerousandblahblahblahbuttthereyougosoareyouin?"

Dawn stared blankly at her friend.

"What?" she said.

"ThethingistheGalaxyisstillcollapsingandtheonlyonesthatcansaveitareusandwehavetogobackintimeand …"

"Wait!" Dawn interrupted. "Slower if possible, please."

Fizz caught her breath and started again.

"Look," she said. "The short version is … the basic problem being … I mean, the main situation is …"

"Oh for God's sake, Fizz. Spit it out!"

"The Galactic Council ordered the Earth's relocation and they did it illegally. Earth should never have been towed away. Now the Galaxy is collapsing in on itself, the Space-Time Vortex is destroying itself, and it's all because, theoretically, it knows that the Earth has been wiped out but, for some reason it can't understand, one human being still exists ..."

"Me."

"You. And, apparently, your little friend over there, Dawn Gray mark two. But that doesn't matter. All the Space-Time Vortex knows is that there is one Earth being alive in the Galaxy. It doesn't care how many alternative versions of it there are.

"So ... in a very big nutshell, there is Galactic confusion. On the one hand, the Earth has been relocated to the bum end of space and the planet itself and everything on it is extinct. On the other hand, a human being still exists in the Galaxy somewhere. How is this possible? The Vortex doesn't care; it's just confused and eventually, if it can't make sense of what's going on, it's going to collapse and the Galaxy will implode."

Dawn felt, somewhere deep in the pit of her stomach, that she should be shocked on hearing this revelation, that she should be stunned and shaken and start panicking, but ... she wasn't. She'd been here before. She'd already heard these things from the Empress Garcea back in the Milky Way Ballroom. She'd come across a lot of weird things since she left Earth the first time; this was no different and it was, she assumed, fixable.

"So, what do we do to stop the Galaxy collapsing?"

"... and every living organism in space and time dying?" Fizz added. "Well, one option is to hunt you down and kill

134

you, which I'm guessing is why our old buddy Mantor is here, on orders from the Galactic Council."

"But we saw him blow himself up," Dawn suddenly said. "Didn't we?"

"He got stuck in a Time Pocket," Fizz replied.

"'Course he did," Dawn said. "Silly me … Time Pocket. Perfect get-out clause for manic robots who are trying to kill me. How couldn't I have known? Do go on, please."

Fizz smiled as she suddenly remembered why she liked Dawn Gray so much. She was a pain sometimes, a little bit whiny, but deep down she was more like Fizz than she knew, or even liked to admit.

"The other alternative is for you and me to travel back in time, back to when the Earth was about to be towed, and stop the relocation happening altogether."

"And what will that achieve?"

"Earth doesn't get towed, doesn't get relocated. No reason for the Space-Time Vortex to get confused. The Earth goes on … the human race goes on … no reason for any problem."

"And how exactly do we stop the Earth getting towed?"

"Leave that to me … I've got the moves." Fizz lied. She didn't really, as yet, have a clue how best to use the TimeEggs to save the Earth.

"I had a feeling you'd say something like that," Dawn replied, shaking her head.

"Look, all we've got to do is get out of here," Fizz went on. "We get out of here and I can get us back in time and stop any of this stuff ever happening. The Earth will be safe, your mum and dad will be safe, you and I will be safe and everything goes back to normal. Every Dawn in the right position in space and time, every Dawn Gray in the right dimension, every Dawn Gray back into *her own life*, and the Galaxy is happy again."

"I can help you." Zak's voice drifted through the darkness as his hand extended through Dawn's bars, taking her hand and holding it as well as his webbed, mechanical fingers could manage. "We should go now," he went on. "Orlak will be asleep. I think you're brave, Dawn Gray," he said, pushing his strange, cloth face against the metal bars of his cage. "I think you're very brave … I admire you and I want to do anything I can to help."

Dawn squeezed Zak's hand and looked deeper into his eyes. She couldn't help feeling a little dizzy; in fact she felt as though she could do anything – even save the Galaxy.

"Thank you," she said. "That means so much to me. I can help you too. I want you to come with us."

"Really?" Zak replied, not believing the words Dawn was saying. "I … I don't know what to say. Nobody's ever really wanted me around before; nobody's ever really cared."

"I want you around," Dawn replied. "I care."

"OH! I think I'm gonna be SICK!" Fizz coughed and started to make fake vomiting sounds as she dropped to her knees in her cage. "That is revolting! Why don't you two get a life? You're killing me here! Pass me a bucket; I'm really gonna chuck up!"

Dawn and Zak couldn't help but smile. They didn't care what Fizz thought; they only knew they wanted to help each other and keep each other safe.

In the shadows of Dawn's cage, however, the other Dawn Gray had woken.

She lay there, perfectly still as she watched Dawn Gray and Zak getting closer, and she envied them. She hated her envy; she hated feeling like this, but she couldn't help it. Dawn Gray was everything she was not – pretty, friendly, with a loving family, well off. She had friends, and now it looked as though she had Zak.

The other Dawn Gray didn't move a muscle; she didn't want anybody to know she was awake. But she watched, her eyes barely open … she watched everything going on around her and she thought about the words Fizz had said …

Every Dawn in the right position in space and time, every Dawn Gray in the right dimension, every Dawn Gray back into her own life.

As she watched … the other Dawn Gray began to hatch a plan of her own.

26

don't wake the neighbours!

The plan was simple: Zak was going to disrupt the electric bars to Fizz's and the two Dawns' cages: the girls were then going to free Zak and the four of them, with Kevin, were going to escape Spectalica-Galactica – out into the open where the Holoship could be activated and take them to freedom.

It was simple, effective and quick.

Everyone was going to play their part. Zak would free the girls, the girls would free Zak. Zak knew his way out of Spectalica-Galactica and Fizz had the Holoship to get them off the planet. The other occupants of the Confinement Zone were sleeping soundly; so as long as they were quiet they would be able to escape unnoticed.

This was the theory ... the plan: and it would have worked had it not been for the faint humming sound that started to come from the darkness.

Zak had released the two Dawns, Fizz and Kevin, and Fizz was busy trying to pick the lock to Zak's solid-barred cage when the noise started. It sounded like a refrigerator motor whirring to life. Everyone looked at each other through the gloom of the Confinement Zone. Some of the other creatures stirred grumpily in their sleep as the whirring sound grew louder and was joined by a rather irritating, high-pitched whistle.

"What is *that*?" Fizz snapped, as she fumbled with the lock to Zak's cage.

"I don't know," Zak replied. "But you'd better be quick, 'cause it's getting louder and I don't wanna be in the middle of an escape attempt when Orlak comes barging in here to find out what the noise is."

"Why is everyone so scared of Orlak?" Fizz said. "You know what he is, don't you?"

Nobody had a chance to answer, because suddenly through the darkness there was movement, and Fizz and Dawn instantly realised where the humming, whirring noise was coming from.

Mantor smashed his armour-clad arm at the bars of his cage. The glowing bars shattered and sparks flew as they broke, but Mantor remained unharmed and unconcerned as he grabbed the first person he could lay his clawed hand on …

Dawn Gray.

"FIZZ!" Dawn screamed as Mantor lifted her from the ground by her neck. "Do something, Fizz! QUICK!"

Fizz left what she was doing and rushed to Dawn, leaving Zak to try and pick the lock himself from inside his cage.

Suddenly, the darkness of the Confinement Zone was alive with noise. The other caged creatures awoke, enraged at the noise that had disturbed them. Glowing bars shook and trembled all around the room. Growls and roars of furious anger filled everyone's heads as the more dangerous captives displayed their fury. There were shrieks and screams of rage, wails and cries all around the room as Fizz stared up at Mantor, wondering just exactly what she was going to do.

From nowhere, Kevin suddenly slammed into Mantor's skull, but all the little rugby ball-shaped robot managed to do was send himself spinning across the room in a daze, as Mantor looked on, no more bothered than he would have been if a fly had brushed his head.

SPACE-TIME MANIPULATOR LOCATED

The message flashed on Mantor's screen.

TERMINATION IMMINENT

Dawn closed her eyes and waited. She could hear the sizzling of the ball of laser fire as it grew once again in Mantor's hand.

And then ... it happened. Nobody really saw exactly how he had done it, but the ball of light in Mantor's hand vanished again, and this time the manic machine froze and tilted his head down, pointing his monitor at the being who was kneeling in front of him.

Zak had inserted his multi-tooled hand into Mantor's midriff, into the control panel that was so well hidden beneath his armour. Mantor wobbled for a few seconds; he seemed almost confused.

"Time to go?" Zak said.

"Time to go," Fizz repeated. "That was very cool, by the way."

"Thanks," Zak replied.

Dawn struggled and strained and managed to pry Mantor's fingers from around her throat. She watched as his armour-clad arms rippled and trembled as though they were made of jelly. It really was the strangest thing. His arms felt soft and cold, almost as though they weren't his.

"What's going on with him?" she asked no one in particular.

"Who gives a poo?" Fizz replied. "We're leaving, now. Oi! Dawn Gray the second! Coming?" The other Dawn nodded her head gently as she watched Mantor struggling to get his bearings and figure out what was happening to him. Fizz turned to where Kevin was floating just a few inches off the ground, looking almost as disorientated as Mantor. "You with us, Kev?"

"I'm all wight!" Kevin replied. "Can we just get out of here?" Fizz turned to Zak, who was holding Dawn's hand tightly.

"Lead the way, Stitch," she said.

Zak hurried them all out, past the shrieking, roaring residents of the Confinement Zone, through the darkness and towards a bulging section of cobweb-covered wall, tucked away in the corner.

"Emergency escape hatch," Zak said, grinning in the darkness. "For Orlak, just in case any of his more dangerous stars ever escaped their cage while he was in here." Zak pushed on the domed section of wall and it seemed to press inwards, as though it wasn't solid. Then part of the wall popped, rumbled and slid to one side, revealing a dirty, dingy tunnel.

Zak pulled Dawn into the tunnel and Fizz and Kevin followed.

The other Dawn Gray hesitated, not sure whether to follow, but as she thought about it Orlak came stomping into the room looking furious.

The other Dawn Gray knew then that now was not the time for her; she didn't want to die here, in the Performers' Confinement Zone of Spectalica-Galactica – not here, not now … not when she had so many things she still wanted to do.

27

the swampland

The moment they emerged from the secret tunnel and into the outside, Fizz, Dawn and everyone else instantly realised that Grakonia is probably the most disgusting, revolting and inhospitable place in the entire Galaxy. To say it was just miles and miles of smelly, boggy swampland and forest would be like saying the Sahara Desert was just *a little bit of sand*.

As soon as they appeared from the tunnel, they found themselves teetering on the narrow bank of a swamp. It was gurgling and bubbling, hissing and spitting, and on the other side, as far as they could see, were miles of thick woodland, trees and shrubbery the likes of which none of them had ever seen. There was no wind on Grakonia; it was far too deep in the outer rim of the Galaxy to receive enough air to generate wind or breezes. Yet inexplicably, the enormous trees, so tall that they seemed to stretch up and up and out into space itself, seemed to move and sway – almost, it seemed, in the direction of the escapees who now stood looking up at them in confused wonder.

"Oh, this is a beautiful place!" Fizz cried. "Really gorgeous; I mean, how is this place not a more popular holiday spot?"

"I told you it was going to be difficult to find a way off Grakonia itself," Zak said to Dawn.

"Yeah, and I told you that I had the moves, didn't I?" Fizz snapped, as she rummaged through her hip-bag and produced the little black box that somehow contained the Holoship. Fizz pulled a slip of folded paper out from the side of the box and unfolded it.

"Instructions," she said, as she realised everyone was nervously watching her. She held the black box out to the other Dawn Gray.

"Hold this a sec, will ya, mate?" The other Dawn Gray took the box from Fizz and held it in her fingertips, keeping it as far away from her face as possible, as though she thought it was some kind of bomb that was about to go off.

Fizz, Dawn, Zak and Kevin turned away from the other Dawn, each of them trying to read and understand the complicated Holoship instructions, so none of them noticed the terrifying beast rearing up from the swamp in front of the other Dawn.

"Er ..." the other Dawn Gray squeaked, frozen with fear as the Aquakon Grakon reared up from the swamp, extending his scaly, horrible hand out to her and trying to reach the odd little black box which had grabbed his curiosity.

"Er ... help?" the other Dawn Gray squeaked again, but still nobody heard her. The others were now arguing amongst themselves as they read and reread the Holoship instructions, trying to figure out the best way to activate it and make their escape.

"Help!" the other Dawn Gray said again, in a tiny, terrified voice. Suddenly the Aquakon hissed and lunged forward, grabbing at her hand. The alternative Dawn Gray shrieked and threw the Holoship into the air, over the Aquakon

Grakon's head and over the swamp itself. It landed with a dull thud on the other side of the swamp, just at the edge of the forest.

"What are you doing?!" Fizz screamed, realising what had happened and seeing where the little black box with the escape ship inside it had landed.

"That thing was gonna eat me!" the other Dawn Gray said, in a trembling voice.

"Don't be soft!" Zak spat. "It's an Aquakon … it can't leave the swamp. It just wanted what you had; it's a scavenger – they're all scavengers, Aquakons. All you had to do was step away from the swamp to where it couldn't reach you!"

"I'm sorry!" the other Dawn Gray said, tears starting to well in her eyes. "I didn't know that!"

"Well, this is great!" Fizz cried out. "Just flipping brilliant! What are we gonna do now?!"

The other Dawn Gray turned away from the others and walked away, crying silently to herself as Fizz, Dawn and Zak carried on arguing about what their next move should be.

Dozens of Aquakon Grakons had now appeared in the swamp, all of them slowly rearing their heads up from below the surface and looking longingly at the mysterious little black box on the opposite bank.

"Man, those things are ugly," Fizz said, watching as more and more Aquakons reared up from the swamp, each of them making the most horrific hissing sound as they gazed at the little black box.

"You reckon they can't leave the swamp?" Fizz asked Zak.

"That's right. These are the elders of Grakonia, the ones who believe all Grakons should live in the swampland; they can't survive outside the swamp."

"Yeah, but there are other Grakons who can live on land," Dawn said.

"Terra Firmakons," Zak said. "The younger Grakons. They have designs on leaving Grakonia one day and venturing out into space, something no Grakon has ever done."

"Right, whatever," Fizz said. "Thanks for the history lessons, Stitch. Fact is … these Terra Firmakons, or whatever you call them, are gonna be looking for us right now, along with Orlak, so we've got to figure a way across this swamp and get to the Holoship."

"Use me," a little voice called out from somewhere behind them.

Fizz, Dawn and Zak turned to see Kevin hovering close by. "I can get you across the swamp," he said with a little flash of his pale blue eyes. "One at a time, of course – but I can help … can't I?"

Nothing more was said; everyone understood what Kevin was saying and everyone knew that he was right.

Dawn was the first to go; she removed her own little black hip-bag from around her waist, threw the handle around Kevin's body and clung onto each end.

A soft peck on the cheek from Zak, which made Dawn blush bright red, and slowly and carefully Kevin rose higher off the ground and began the journey across the hissing, bubbling swamp.

It only took a minute for Kevin to reach the other side. He hovered lower and Dawn breathed a sigh of relief as her feet touched the solid, if a little earthy, ground. She left the bag draped over Kevin's body and he returned for his next passenger: the other Dawn Gray.

In no time at all, both Dawns were safely on the other side of the swamp.

Zak was next.

He took a tight hold of the bag and Kevin began to carry him across to where the two Dawns stood and watched nervously.

And then … it happened.

Fizz noticed it first but she was not quick enough to understand exactly what it was she had seen, and therefore was not quick enough to scream a warning to Kevin and Zak.

The Aquakon Grakons were beginning to bob up and down in the swamp as they peered longingly up at Zak and Kevin hovering above them. Clearly, their interest in the little black box had now faded somewhat; there was a new, more interesting distraction – one that the Aquakons could reach and get their hands on and they looked intent on making sure they got it.

Zak screamed out in surprise and terror as he looked down at the huge, black, glassy eyes of the Grakon snarling and growling at his ankle.

From the swampland below came hundreds of ear-piercing cries and whistles as Grakons appeared all over the place, each of them leaping and bounding up out of the swamp and splashing back in with a rather swampy-sounding *plop*.

Dawn and Dawn were screaming from the other side of the swamp for Kevin to hurry.

Kevin tried to fly higher, away from the leaping, snarling Aquakon Grakons as they stretched and lunged for Zak. But the combined weight of Zak and the Grakon attached to him was too much and, slowly but ever so terribly surely, he began to lose height and fall closer and closer to the swamp and the hundreds of aquatic monsters that were waiting below.

The Grakons reared their heads above the surface of the swamp and repeated their piercing, bone-chilling chant as they waited for their victims to fall within their reach. The Grakon still attached to Zak was tugging and hissing wildly, trying to loosen Zak's grip and pull him down into the swamp.

"Fizz!" Dawn screamed from the other side of the swamp. "Do something!"

"Like what!?" Fizz bellowed back.

"I don't know! Anything!"

Fizz stared out at the swamp and at Kevin and Zak, who were now just a fingertip out of reach from the hundreds of wild, savage Grakons.

She thought.

She thought about TimeEggs. She could use one, but she wasn't really sure how best to use it and they were, after all, valuable; she didn't really think, considering that she had lost two already, she should risk losing another one.

No, there was only one option. It was risky, it was dangerous – in fact it was downright silly and highly idiotic, but there was no other way Fizz could see of saving Kevin and Zak.

Fizz eyed up the situation before her. Kevin was only a couple of feet from the bank of the swamp and from the two Dawn Grays. The Grakons all had their heads above the surface of the swamp.

She didn't really have any more time to think about it: some of the Aquakon Grakons' scaly, bony fingers were reaching up towards Zak's ankles, trying to get hold of his leg to pull him down below the surface of the swamp. She had to move now; she just had to do it.

She took a careful look, calculated the number of Grakons heads above the surface of the swamp and their positions, took a deep breath – and leapt into the swamp.

28

mantor's troubles

Orlak had already given chase. Accompanied by a small army of Terra Firmakon Grakons, he was crossing the woodland of Grakonia in search of the escapees.

Mantor was in pursuit too, but as he stomped through the boggy woodland, his heavy feet shaking the ground as he went, he was struggling with the strange things that had begun to happen to him.

A deep, sorrowful moan was grumbling from beneath the monitor embedded in his skull, and at times he seemed to be staggering across Grakonia like a wounded animal, rather than stomping along like the focused machine he once had been.

There were sounds all around him. There was screaming coming from a short way to his left, through some trees. The Earth girl and her friends, perhaps? Mantor could hear the army of Grakons, too, as they pursued the Earth girl. Orlak was nearer, Mantor knew that, but there was nothing he could do to change it. He was becoming disorientated, confused. The armour of his enormous frame felt soft and his programmed task was mixed up.

I AM MANTOR

a message flashed on his screen.

I SEEK THE SPACE-TIME MANIPULATOR

TERMINATION MUST BE ACHIEVED

I AM MANTOR

I AM ...

I AM ...

And then a new message appeared on Mantor's bandaged screen: a message, a program, maybe – certainly something Mantor had never come across before.

It simply read:

ERROR. ERROR. ERROR. ERROR. ERROR. ERROR. ERROR. ERROR.

MALFUNCTION HAS OCCURRED.

MAINFRAME SYSTEM SHUTDOWN IN T-MINUS 30 SECONDS.

Mantor froze. He didn't even wobble or tremble. As he stood in the gloomy light of Grakonia, surrounded by the swampland and forests, he looked like a gigantic, hideous mannequin.

A new message appeared:

MAINFRAME SYSTEM SHUTDOWN IN T-MINUS 15 SECONDS.

ORGANIC GENETIC CODE CORRUPTED.

**ORGANIC GENETIC CODE
REPROGRAMMING IN PROGRESS.**

**MAINFRAME SYSTEM SHUTDOWN
IN T-MINUS 5 SECONDS.**

4 ...

3 ...

2 ...

1 ...

SHUTDOWN.

Mantor fell forward. Nothing could stop his gigantic, heavy, metal body from crashing to the swampy, boggy ground, with a Grakonia-shuddering crash that was heard for miles around.

His monitor was blank.

He did not move.

Mantor just lay there, screen-down in the filthy swampland – and he did not appear to be getting up again.

29

the amazing
disappearing holoship

It looked quite stunning. It looked highly impressive and incredibly heroic. In fact, had it not been for the bursts of screaming and her cries of "Oh poo!", "Oh blimey!" and "HELP!" Fizz's Grakon head-dance would have been, possibly, the coolest thing anyone had ever seen.

As it was, however, it was only mildly impressive and actually looked a rather stupid and suicidal thing to do.

Fizz bounded from one Grakon to the next, hopping and stepping onto each of their heads, her arms outstretched to help her balance, as she danced her way across them towards Kevin and Zak.

Each Grakon let out a wail of grunting rage as Fizz landed a combat-booted foot on each of their heads, plunging them back below the surface of the swamp.

When Zak was within lunging distance she leapt from the last Grakon head, dived through the air, grabbed hold of Zak around the waist, planting both her booted feet on the Grakon that was pulling at Zak's head, sending him back into the swamp, and then swung herself and Zak towards the safety of the bank.

The pair landed with a dull thud as Kevin, the weight of Zak suddenly released from him, shot into the air as though he were a balloon that had just had all the air let out of it.

Dawn scooped Zak up from the ground and hugged him tightly as Kevin plummeted down, only stopping himself just a few inches from the ground.

"Don't worry 'bout me!" Fizz called, as she dragged herself to her feet. "I'm fine, no worries." Dawn and Zak smiled at Fizz and then at Kevin.

"Thank you," Zak said. There was a sincerity in his eyes that was unmistakeable, at least to Dawn. Clearly, Zak was not used to people risking their lives to save him. After all, Dawn thought, he wasn't used to anyone even wanting to talk to him or look at him, let alone endangering themselves for him. Dawn thought that Zak wasn't really sure how to show his gratitude.

"I'm not really used to people being nice to me and you two …" – he turned to Dawn, "and you, Dawn, have … well, you've done more for me in the last few hours than anyone ever has in my entire life."

"Please!" Fizz cried out. "Enough with the squishy stuff; you're making me wanna be sick again." She turned to Kevin and rubbed his shiny, metallic body. "You okay, Kev?"

Kevin's eyes flashed a pale blue.

"That was fun," he said. "I don't ever want to do anything like that ever again. But it was fun."

Everyone looked out at the swampland. The Grakons were poking their hideous, scaly heads out of the water just far enough to snarl and hiss at them.

Fizz picked up the little black box containing the Holoship.

"Right then, kiddies!" Fizz bellowed as she jumped to her feet. "Enough of Grakon history, interesting as it is, I'm sure. We outsmarted 'em, so let them hit and spit in their filthy little swamp all they want. So long as they can't get to us, that's sweet with me. Shall we move on? Yes? Good. Time to go, I think. Everyone ready?"

Dawn looked across at her other self. The other Dawn Gray was quiet, even a little different somehow. She stood a few feet away from Dawn and seemed to be avoiding her eyes.

"Ready to start again … *Dawn*?" Dawn said, smiling.

The other Dawn Gray stared off into space but replied, in a whisper: "Sure."

Fizz pushed a little red button on the black box and tossed it onto the ground. In a flash of light the ship shot out of its box on a beam of light, and began hovering and revolving in mid-air right in front of everyone's eyes.

Nobody moved.

"Now what?" Dawn said.

"Hang on." Fizz produced the little slip of paper from her pocket and unfolded it. "Instructions for boarding and programming the Holoship." Fizz began reading down the paper, her eyes flitting from left to right, mumbling to herself incoherently as she read. The others looked on nervously, even more nervously when the Holoship stopped revolving and seemed to angle itself upwards towards space.

"Uh … Fizz?" Dawn said.

"Boarding a Holoship is simple," Fizz read aloud. "Simply walk into the desired area of the ship; its holographic form means no doors are either visible or needed."

"Fizz?" Dawn said again, but Fizz didn't hear.

"Once inside a Holoship, the interior of the craft becomes and appears as solid as any normal ship. Warning …" Fizz trailed off into silence.

"Fizz!" Dawn cried.

"Oh dear," Fizz said to herself. "Warning. Be ready to board the Holoship before you activate it. Once activated, the Holoship will leave on its already pre-programmed course in ten seconds."

In another flash of light, the Holoship was gone.

"Oh poo," Fizz said.

30

fizz's brief goodbye

"We have a problem," Fizz said, solemnly. "A big, *big* problem."

Suddenly, the other Dawn Gray flung herself at Fizz, clinging to her leg in a hysterical fit of panic and tears.

"You're unbelievable, you know that?"

Fizz looked up as she tried to shake the screaming girl from her leg, and saw Dawn glaring at her. It took a moment for Fizz to understand exactly the look Dawn was giving her. Considering that she had just leapt across a dozen deadly Grakon heads to save her boyfriend, Fizz thought Dawn would have looked and sounded a little more grateful. Instead, Fizz found herself looking into Dawn's eyes and seeing a look of desperation, frustration and anger.

"You have a point you'd like to make to the whole class, Gray?"

"Can't you just stop joking around for five minutes?" Dawn cried. "We're in trouble here, Fizz ... *serious* trouble, and all you can do is stand there, make smart remarks and mess about. So those Aquakon Grakons in the swamp can't or won't come on land – so what? There are a lot of ... "

"Terra Firmakon Grakons," Zak said.

"Right … Terra Firmakon Grakons," Dawn went on. "Grakons that *do* come on land, and Orlak is gonna be looking for us. We're in serious, big-time trouble here, and you've just blown our only chance of getting off this planet!"

"I see," Fizz said, calmly. "You're not happy with the way I've risked my life, *again*, to save you. You're not happy with the way I've just zipped halfway across the Galaxy, *again*, to find you. You're not happy that without me turning up, *again*, you'd probably, almost certainly, be in a lot more trouble than you are now. Is that right?"

Dawn looked across at Zak and her other self for encouragement, but neither of them seemed to offer any. Dawn realised at that moment that this was a clash of personalities between herself and Fizz – a clash that only the two of them understood. Maybe Dawn's alternative self felt it, but it was hard to tell; she was sitting on a tree stump staring out at the swamp, and didn't seem to be aware of anything or anyone around her.

"I'm not saying that, Fizz," Dawn finally answered. "I'm just saying …"

Dawn was silent, unable to finish the sentence.

Fizz raised her eyebrows expectantly, waiting for Dawn to finish what she was saying.

The truth was, however, that Dawn Gray didn't know how to finish the sentence, and even if she were given the rest of eternity to think of a way to finish it, she still didn't think she would be able to.

It was difficult, after all, her relationship with Fizz. It was complicated, confusing … *problematic*.

It was true that Fizz had saved Dawn's life on a number of occasions – the biggest time, of course, being when the Earth was towed away and relocated by the Trygonian Council Recovery Vessel. Fizz had been a friend of Dawn's for a while before that fateful night. The two of them had become quite close at school. Fizz was quirky, strange, different – nothing like Dawn's other friends: all they ever talked about was boys and make-up and going out and the latest fashions and latest tunes in the charts.

Fizz wasn't like that, never had been, even before things got … well, weird and the Earth was towed away. But that was what had brought them so close together. Fizz was different, unique, and Dawn liked that about her.

On the other hand, even though Fizz had saved Dawn's life, and they had been friends long before they ventured into outer space together, it could be argued that the reason Fizz had to keep rescuing Dawn and travelling across space and time to find her was because she kept getting them into trouble in the first place.

Everything Fizz did, everything she touched, went wrong.

When they first DROSSed off the Earth, she had landed herself and Dawn on an alternative Earth populated by killer, mutant dogs. Then she had led them right into the hands of Mantor and, after all that, Fizz had finally dumped Dawn on a planet full of thousands of other Dawn Grays, Dawn Grays who were all as frustrated and angry with Fizz as Dawn herself was – as, indeed, she still was and was feeling right at this very moment.

"You're an idiot!" Dawn spat. It was a hateful, horrible thing to say, and deep down she really, *really* hadn't meant to say it. It just kind of exploded out of her.

Zak looked at Dawn in shock; Kevin's little blue eyes faded to a dim shade of grey. Even the other Dawn Gray managed to raise her eyes and look in the direction the outburst had come from.

Dawn was amazed to see that, for the first time since she had known her, Fizz actually looked hurt.

"Fine," she said, gravely. "You feel like that? I'll go then." Fizz walked away from the others, towards the forest behind them. "I'll stay out of your way from now on, Dawn Gray. You think you can take better care of yourself and sort this whole mess out? You think you can save the Earth, save the entire Galaxy and every being in it all by yourself? Then go ahead: be my guest and try it. Personally, I never wanted the job of looking after your sorry backside anyway, so actually you're doing me a favour."

Fizz walked to the edge of the forest.

"Fizz," Dawn called. "Please, I … I didn't mean it. I'm … I'm sorry."

"Goodbye, Dawn. Goodbye, everyone," Fizz said, not looking back. "I'll lose myself in these woods. In this forest. We won't ever run across each other again, I promise you. Not in any other time, not in any other dimension." Fizz walked into the woods. As she disappeared behind the mass of trees she whispered. "You'll never hear from me … ever again."

The others, Dawn and Dawn, Kevin and Zak, didn't know where to look or what to say. Dawn, for one, couldn't help feeling she had done something terrible – made a horrible mistake that she knew she would never be able to correct or make up for. She had hurt Fizz, crushed her, destroyed her feelings and her emotions. And for what ... Pride? Anger?

How stupid was that?

Was Fizz really that bad after all? Dawn couldn't really answer 'yes' to that question. Sure, she had made mistakes, endangered them both from time to time; but in the end her mistakes were only in the course of her looking out for Dawn and trying to keep her safe and protected.

Dawn hated herself more the longer she stood at the bank of the swamp, thinking about what she had just done and said. She couldn't imagine never seeing Fizz again, not having her help, never hearing from her again.

In actual fact, however, Dawn did hear from Fizz again ... about seven seconds after Fizz had disappeared into the forest, her voice came drifting back to the bank of the swamp.

"Uh ... sorry to bother you all, I know what I just said back there and everything, but ... could someone help me please? I think I'm a bit stuck and about to be a bit dead."

31

grakonia – alive!

The Dawns, Kevin and Zak raced into the forest, leaving the swamp behind them. Even just a short way in, the world of Grakonia seemed different amongst the vegetation. The ground was firmer and harder and the trees, which climbed high up into the blackness of space, all seemed in some very peculiar way to be leaning in towards the strangers to Grakonia – almost as though they were watching them and following them.

They found Fizz hanging upside down in the air. She seemed to be caught up in some dead branches belonging to one of the trees.

"Fizz?" Dawn exclaimed. "What …?"

Dawn didn't manage to get another word out. Her feet were suddenly swept away from beneath her as something rough and spiky wrapped itself tightly around her ankles and pulled her feet out from under her. Dawn hit the ground with a thump and screamed, as whatever it was that had a hold of her dragged her along the forest floor a short way, and then began hoisting her into the air by her ankles.

Dawn's pyjamas tore and ripped around her arms and after just a few surprising, unnerving and, to be honest, thoroughly terrifying seconds, she found herself hanging upside down in the air, swinging slowly back and forth right next to where Fizz was hanging.

"So … you were saying?" Fizz said, quite calmly, looking across at Dawn. "I was an idiot?"

"Sorry about that," Dawn replied, honestly. "I didn't mean it; you know I didn't."

"Of course I know," Fizz said, with a grin. "You just walked into the same trap I did. And *I m* an idiot?"

"Trap?" Dawn repeated.

"The trees," Fizz replied, in a low whisper. "They don't seem to want to let us go anywhere."

Dawn looked down (that is to say, she looked *up*) at her feet and followed the spiky-looking branches that were wrapped around her ankles. They led down, twisting and writhing around towards the ground, to the base of one of the giant trees.

The tree itself was leaning further towards Dawn and Fizz. It was actually moving and creaking as its huge, heavy trunk leaned closer.

Dawn stared at the enormous trunk as she felt its branches around her ankles tighten, and thought, for the briefest of seconds, that she saw it blink.

"Did that tree just …"

"Blink?" Fizz finished. "I thought so too! Cool, huh?"

Suddenly, the whole forest began to move and shake and shudder. The first thought that went through Dawn's mind was that it was an earthquake, but then she saw what the trees were doing.

All over the place roots were sprouting up from the ground below. The trees themselves began moaning and groaning out loud, as their foundations snapped and cracked. The roots whipped around everyone, some of them hooking themselves around the other Dawn's body, others grappling Zak's ankles. Some even flew through the air and wrapped themselves, vice-like, around Kevin's little metal body.

The forest of Grakonia was alive. The eyes in the trees opened and were fierce and angry as they locked onto their strange, uninvited visitors and bound them with their deadly roots.

In just a matter of seconds Dawn, Dawn, Fizz, Zak and Kevin were all tangled, caught and snared in thorny, spiky roots, hanging helplessly in the air, dangling between the great, monstrous trees of Grakonia.

"Okay!" Fizz called out through a mouthful of roots which had entwined themselves around her head. "Any ideas!? This would be a good time to speak up!"

Nobody said anything.

"No one?!" Fizz called out. "Sure? No ideas? No suggestions? No escape plans?"

Silence.

"Blimey, you lot are a fat load of help, eh?"

The forest of Grakonia had fallen silent too. The roots and branches continued to constrict around their new prey, but the trees themselves seemed to have become still again.

"What do they want?" the other Dawn said, in a trembling voice.

"My guess?" Fizz replied. "We're not actually welcome in the forest, and this is the trees' way of letting us know that."

"So … it's a warning then?" the other Dawn said, hopefully. "They'll make their warning and then let us go, right?"

Fizz thought for a moment before replying.

"Um … no: they're going to kill us, Dawn the second. They're going to squeeze us and squeeze us with these horrible prickly root things of theirs until we're dead. Kinda like juicing an orange, see?"

Silence again.

The roots that were coiled around everyone multiplied and tightened and, in just a few minutes, the five found themselves completely wrapped in the prickly roots of the deadly Grakonian trees.

And there they all hung, helpless, trapped and slowly being strangled.

Then out of the silence there came a rather odd sound, a little bit like something being shot through the air. Not a bullet or a laser blast, but something hard and long, like an arrow from a bow. Another of the odd sounds immediately followed and then another, and then another. The trees seemed to tilt backwards and began making the weirdest sound, as if they were in pain. And then Dawn Gray plummeted to the ground. Still wrapped in the roots, she hit the ground with a bone-shaking crunch. Zak fell to the ground just beside her, followed by Fizz and then the other Dawn and, just a few seconds later, Kevin joined them.

Dawn, Dawn, Zak and Fizz pulled the dead tree roots from their bodies and Fizz and Dawn helped Kevin to unravel himself.

"How cool was that?" Fizz said, cheerfully, as she held up two dead ends of the deadly roots. "They've been cut clean in two; someone's looking out for us."

"Yeah … but who?" Dawn replied, nervously looking through the trees.

Fizz turned round and was faced with a sight so terrifying that she almost wished she was back hanging upside down in the trees.

"Oh …" Fizz said.

"Poo," Dawn finished.

Before them stood Orlak, tall and spindly, looking as evil and vicious as ever, and with him, an army, a battalion, almost an entire planet's population, of Terra Firmakon Grakons.

32

orlak uncovered

The huge number of Grakons seemed content, for the time being at least, to let Orlak approach Fizz, Dawn and the others alone.

He crept forward, long, freakish limbs testing the terrain as he stepped closer, his hideous face leering and salivating as he crept.

"Nak-tilla, NAK-TAA!" Orlak spat, casting his evil-looking eyes over each one of his escapees. "You have caused much trouble for me tonight. It is lucky that you are all such prized attractions at my Spectalica-Galactica; if you were not, I could simply hand you over to the Grakons. They wish, I believe, to boil your bones and make some kind of stew with your remains. Apparently, all of you would feed most of this planet's population for a month!"

Dawn, Dawn and Zak recoiled slightly as Orlak crept closer still. Kevin stayed hovering quite a way up in the air, out of reach of even Orlak's long grasp.

Fizz on the other hand, did not move a muscle.

"Listen, lanky," she said curtly, as Dawn and the others gasped and clung onto each other anxiously. Surely Fizz was not going to endanger them all by mocking Orlak the Great?

"The bottom line? You're ugly. You smell – *bad*. Your show sucks – only creatures as dumb as this load of Grakons here are capable of enjoying it. And you, my skinny, ugly little friend, are a fake."

"Er … Fizz," Dawn said, tentatively. "I think that's enough; you've said your piece, okay? Let's just go with Orlak quietly. There'll be other chances to escape."

Fizz snapped round to face Dawn and gasped.

"Are you two holding hands?" She was looking at Dawn and Zak; their hands were clasped together tightly, their fingers interlocking. "Seriously, you two. I'm sure it's love and all that, but we've got a situation here. Can't you leave each other alone for one minute?"

"NAK-TAA!" Orlak screamed angrily behind them.

"Oi!" Fizz screamed back at him. "Button it, will ya? I'm talking here!"

"Fizz!" Dawn bellowed. "What are you doing? He'll kill us!"

"Or he'll turn us over to the Grakons," Zak added.

"This bloke?" Fizz said, smiling. "Orlak the Great?"

Everyone turned to Orlak, expecting him to fly at Fizz in a terrible rage – but, unbelievably, he actually looked … well, a little bit nervous.

"See …" Fizz went on, as she started edging towards Orlak. "I know exactly what you are, matey. That makes you nervous, doesn't it?"

"NAK-TAA!" Orlak screamed, a little less convincingly this time.

"Yeah, yeah, yeah," Fizz laughed. "Nak-taa to you, too." Fizz stepped closer and closer to Orlak, and the others were amazed to see him actually retreating a few steps.

"You see, I know that not many people know what you really are. I know that for years and years now, you've been faking it as some big-time, terrifying ringleader of Spectalica-Galactica. I know all about you, Orlak my man."

Suddenly, Fizz lunged at Orlak. He tried to scramble away from her grasping arms, but the Grakons behind him blocked his way. Fizz grabbed the collar of his long overcoat and pulled, and in one swift movement the coat fell away from his body revealing …

… a teeny, tiny little spider.

With a very big head.

And ridiculously long legs.

"WHAT!?" Dawn cried.

"IS!" Zak added.

"THAT?" the other Dawn finished.

"That, ladies and gentlemen," Fizz announced. "Is Arachnacabuus-Mutantae. In other words, to you and me … a spider with a big head and long legs."

The Grakons were shoving each other and poking each other in curious amazement as they stared at Orlak. Orlak the Great had collapsed onto the ground on all *eight* of his legs. His head was still the size of a normal head and his legs were extraordinarily long, but his body was no bigger than a common or garden house spider and, without his long, reinforced overcoat to help him stand upright, the only way

Orlak could move now was by scurrying around on the floor like any normal spider.

"He's a mutant," Fizz went on explaining. Now the Grakons seemed to be listening as intently as everyone else, though whether they could understand what Fizz was saying wasn't clear.

"The first arachnid in the Galaxy to develop vocal abilities and gene mutations of various parts of the body, namely his stupid fat head and his ridiculously long legs. He's a con artist, a fraudster – nothing more than a big, fat fake."

Orlak began scurrying away through the trees, and for a moment some of the Grakons, furious that they had paid so many Daktaa to Orlak over the years to see Spectalica-Galactica, when all they really had to do was step on him or put a big glass over him and throw him in the forest somewhere, seemed to consider giving chase.

But they didn't move.

"Go get him!" Fizz cried out to the Grakons. "Go find him. I'm sure he won't have any arguments about handing over the running of Spectalica-Galactica to you all now! Go on! You'll be famous! You'll all be rich!"

The Grakons didn't move.

They had no interest in running Spectalica-Galactica.

They had no interest in travelling the Galaxy with the show.

They had no interest in being rich.

But, the Grakons did have an interest – in fact, a particular passion for ...

"Stew," Dawn said to herself.

"What?" Fizz said snapping her head round to face her friend.

"I think …" Dawn went on, "they still want their stew."

The Grakons, slowly but ever so deliberately, began moving towards Fizz and the others. They were armed with various sharp-looking spears and other pointy things, which were held in different kinds of pouches and holsters and backpacks.

"Maybe they'd like an omelette," Fizz said, in a low whisper.

"What?" Dawn replied.

"An omelette," Kevin repeated, giggling. "That's a good one."

"Know what you need to make an omelette?" Fizz said to the others. Dawn, Dawn and Zak stared at Fizz in disbelief. Their escape from Spectalica-Galactica had been one disastrous encounter after another and now here they were, it seemed, finally facing death. No more ways out, nobody else around to save their necks, and pretty much the entire population of armed and dangerous, scaly-looking Grakons marching towards them looking very, very hungry. And Fizz was talking about the various different ways they could be about to be consumed.

"Eggs," Fizz said. She rummaged through her bag and produced … the last two TimeEggs. She held them up in the air.

"Behold, Grakons!" she said, very loudly and clearly, as if she were holding up something extraordinarily beautiful and precious. The Grakons froze and stared at the TimeEggs in Fizz's hand.

"Watch and learn."

Fizz cracked one of the TimeEggs on the side of a tree, which grumbled and moaned as she did so. After apologising to the tree, Fizz tossed the two halves of the TimeEgg into the air, trying to throw the halves as far apart as possible.

The Grakons watched, unimpressed.

"Very valuable," Fizz said. "Would bring many people to your world in search of them: many people, many beings, many creatures ... many great stews, huh?"

The Grakons were confused and Fizz, now more than ever, was beginning to realise that the Grakons couldn't understand a word she was saying.

"Kev!" She called out. "Visual demonstration, if you please."

"What?" Kevin hovered down beside Fizz's head. "I don't want to go into that thing again. It was howwible."

"Kevin," Fizz said, sternly. "We're about to be mashed up into stew here; you wanna complain later? Get into the space between the TimeEggs and show these scaly pains in the bum what it does. Don't worry, we'll all be right behind you."

"I weally don't think that's fair, do you?" Kevin protested. "Why can't Dawn go? Or the other Dawn even? She doesn't say much after all; she wouldn't be missed awound here. Let her go. I weally don't see why I should GOOOOOOOOOOOOOOO!"

A little shove, in fact an almighty push from Fizz, and Kevin had shot into the gap between the TimeEggs, vanishing into thin air. The Grakons gasped with terror and wonder as they stared at the space of seemingly normal air between the two halves of the TimeEgg.

"One more left!" Fizz called out, holding up the last TimeEgg. "Who wants it, huh? Cool toy, isn't it? You could trade for it, make stews with it – anything you like." She tilted her head to the side and whispered out of the corner of her mouth:

"Go."

Then she turned her face back towards the Grakons, who were steadily moving towards her again, their expression greedy and hungry now. Clearly they had plans of stealing the last TimeEgg from Fizz and then, afterwards, having their stew anyway.

"Any bidders!? Come on now, who wants this little egg and all its wonderful tricks!?" She turned to face the others.

"Follow Kevin!" she screamed at them.

The other Dawn Gray, without a moment's hesitation, sprinted towards the space between the TimeEgg halves and vanished through it.

Now the Grakons seemed alert. They suddenly seemed to cotton on to what was happening and knew, instantly, that they were about to be conned.

"Isn't that the last TimeEgg?" Dawn said in a low voice.

"Yes, it is," Fizz said. "And I need it – *we* need it – to save the Galaxy; so if you don't mind, get lost, so I can get out of here before the Grakons get this thing and then my body for some nice Grakonian homemade stew. So GO!"

Dawn leapt through the space in time after Kevin and the other Dawn, with Zak close behind her.

Fizz was about to throw herself after him when, from nowhere, one of the enormous Grakons lunged at her. Flying through the air he smacked her hand, sending the

TimeEgg flying through the air and back towards the swamp.

It all happened in an instant, really. Dawn was through the space between the TimeEgg halves, Zak had just one leg through, and Fizz was watching in horror as the last TimeEgg flew towards the swamp and the waiting Aquakon Grakons who had reared their heads above the surface of the swamp and were waiting, excitedly, to catch hold of whatever treasure it was that was now flying towards them.

With it, Fizz knew, the life of every being in the Galaxy would be lost.

But the Aquakon Grakons did not catch the TimeEgg. Neither did the Terra Firmakon Grakons.

The hand that caught the TimeEgg, in actual fact, belonged to Zak.

From his place half in and half out of times and dimensions, he had thrown out his extendible arm, flung it out to the middle of the swamp and plucked the TimeEgg out of the air.

"That was cool," Fizz said, smiling.

"Catch," Zak said and, with a gentle flick of his nimble, metallic fingers; he zipped the TimeEgg back through the air and into Fizz's hands. The Grakons immediately began making a move towards Fizz again, but she was too fast. She sprinted at the space in time between the TimeEgg halves.

"Go!" she screamed at Zak. "Get in!"

She came to a screeching halt.

Just inside the rift in time, Fizz could see Dawn, still waiting on the very edge, the brink of another time, another dimension. She looked confused, puzzled and a little afraid.

Something was wrong.

"What's going on?" Fizz said.

The space between the TimeEgg halves was brilliant white, a portal to another time and dimension. Where exactly no one knew, but it would certainly lead them away from Grakonia, away from the Grakons intent on boiling them up, and would let them set about making plans to save the Galaxy and the Earth.

But at that very moment, no one was going anywhere and Fizz couldn't understand why

She looked at Dawn, teetering on the edge of two dimensions.

Behind her, she heard the wailing and excitable screams of the Aquakon Grakons. She looked at Zak; he looked scared.

Fizz felt through the ground, beneath her feet, the thundering of the other Grakons racing back towards her, intent on getting their large, scaly hands on the TimeEgg, and on her.

Fizz didn't have a clue what was happening. And then …

"Sorry," Zak said, in a soft, scared little whisper – and Fizz knew.

She knew that Zak wasn't coming with them

She knew the adventure, for him, stopped here.

She knew … the Grakons had him.

33

and then ...
there were four

"NO!" Dawn screamed, but Fizz knew it was no use.

Zak tried to pull his arm back but it wouldn't budge. Fizz looked out at the swamp and saw several of the Aquakon Grakons pulling and yanking on Zak's arm, trying to pull him in.

Zak smiled at Fizz.

"Nice knowing you," he said, faintly.

Fizz had never felt so helpless, so utterly useless, as Zak was literally dragged off his feet and pulled, bit by bit, towards the swamp. The other Grakons were still racing at Fizz; they had been momentarily distracted by the jeers and screams of their aquatic brothers, but now they were heading right for Fizz again and the last TimeEgg.

Fizz looked back at the swamp, trying to catch a glimpse of Zak, but it was too late. He was gone.

She turned back to the void between the TimeEgg shells and, resting her fingertip on the one half of the shell, she leapt into the gap in time.

As Fizz jumped through, she flicked her finger against the shell of the TimeEgg and it fell to the floor and shattered.

The Grakons raced past the spot where the gap in time had just been, a split second before, and for some bizarre reason (they weren't the most intelligent creatures in the Galaxy) they just kept running.

34

species undefined

Orlak squealed, the breath leaving his body in tiny, exasperated gasps that were all that he could make through the vice-like grip which held him.

His long, spindly legs splayed and swung all around his tiny body as the grip tightened and tightened until finally, Orlak slumped lifeless on the sodden, boggy ground of Grakonia.

Beside Orlak's still body, Mantor stirred.

His enormous, hulking metal body was weak and heavy, but there was a new message flashing on his screen:

ORGANIC GENETIC CODE
REPROGRAMMING COMPLETE.

SPECIES REDEFINED.

STATE BEING ...

Then, there was nothing. The screen flashed the same message:

STATE BEING ...

STATE BEING ...

STATE BEING ...

But no answer came.

Slowly, Mantor hauled himself to his feet and stood shakily amidst the darkness of the Grakonian night.

STATE BEING ...

Mantor looked down at his long, armour-plated arms, his clawed, black hands and the control panels and switches that were moulded and fused to his chest and forearms.

STATE BEING ...

He reached up a hand and rubbed his fingers across the smooth surface of the monitor buried beneath the rags and bandages. He turned his head in the direction of Orlak's lifeless body, lying on the ground beside him.

I AM ...

his message began in response to the question.

... MANTOR

he finished.

A new message flashed across Mantor's monitor in response.

NEGATIVE.

ORGANIC GENETIC CODE
REPROGRAMMING COMPLETE.

SPECIES REDEFINED.

SPECIES UNKNOWN.
SPECIES UNDEFINED.

STATE BEING ...

Mantor wobbled again, seemingly a little unsure of himself. From behind his monitor a deep, rumbling growl and groan emitted.

STATE BEING ...

the message ran once again, and this time Mantor answered.

I ...

... DO NOT KNOW.

35

inside the timeegg

How I wish I could tell you that everything about the Galaxy and about time and space was wonderful, magical and full of adventure.

Alas, however, I can't do that. There are some things in the Galaxy and in the whole twisted, confused and completely bizarre business of space and time travel that are just bland, ordinary, thoroughly dull and, to be perfectly honest with you, just as boring and infuriating as any banal and arduous task you might have to perform in your own daily lives.

For instance, waiting in a doctor's surgery.

Waiting at a bus stop.

Queuing in general.

All boring, I'm sure you agree. All time-consuming and thoroughly aggravating and annoying.

Unfortunately, reader, passage through the wonders of the TimeEgg time and space void is just as dull as any of those things. In fact, it is simply one big queue.

I will attempt to be as brief as possible.

"I can't believe he's gone," Dawn muttered to herself. Tears were welling in her eyes and she was physically shaking. Kevin looked as though he was about to cry, too. The other Dawn was trying not to meet anyone's eyes; and Fizz … well, Fizz was feeling extremely uncomfortable with the whole situation.

"No one ever really dies, Dawn," she said awkwardly, as she tried to pat her friend comfortingly on the shoulder. "You know that by now. Another time, another dimension maybe … who knows? You'll run into him again."

Dawn tried a smile, but it was forced and faded instantly.

"He died saving us, Fizz," she whimpered. "I hardly knew him and he died saving me … us, all of us!"

"Well, yeah, that was nice of him, I s'pose," Fizz replied.

"You!" A voice spat from somewhere. Dawn and Fizz looked up to find the other Dawn glaring at them.

"What?" Fizz said.

"What do you mean?" Dawn added.

"Let's not kid ourselves here," the other Dawn said. "That … robot thing died for you. No one else."

"What are you saying?" asked Dawn, heat rising in her face, anger beginning to bubble from somewhere: she wasn't sure where from or for what reason exactly.

The alternative Dawn Gray bit down on her lip, tears welling in her own eyes as she stared at Dawn and Fizz. She looked as though she was about to burst, as if she had a million and one other things to say. But in the end she regained her composure and turned away from them.

"Nothing," she said. "Forget it."

Fizz and Kevin exchanged a nervous look, both sensing that they had just avoided what could have turned out to be a rather unpleasant argument.

"Right, then," Fizz chirped, trying to lighten the mood and taking in her surroundings. "Where the heck are we?"

Dawn, Dawn, Fizz and Kevin looked all around them, each suddenly aware of their stunningly dull surroundings.

White walls.

White floors.

White ceiling.

And ahead of them was one long queue, standing in which were some of the strangest-looking creatures in the Galaxy (although strange did not come as any great shock to anyone by now).

Next to Fizz was a ticket machine, which had a sign above it that read:

THIS IS A TICKET MACHINE

And another sign beneath that, which read:

PLEASE TAKE A TICKET

Fizz took a ticket. On it was written the number – **77486**.

They all looked down the long queue. At the end was a desk, above which was another sign that read:

CUSTOMER SERVICE

Beneath that was another sign, which read:

NOW SERVING ... 3

"Now serving 3!?" Dawn exclaimed. "We're number 77,486! You mean there's 77,483 people before us?"

Fizz looked at Dawn quite calmly.

"Well done, Dawn," she said. "Did you work that sum out all by yourself?"

"What do we do?" Dawn asked, ignoring Fizz's cutting remark.

"Looks like we wait," Fizz replied.

"Wait?" Dawn began screaming again. Her outbursts were beginning to draw some discerning and disgruntled looks from other beings in the otherwise silent room. "With a Galaxy to save? Haven't you got any better ideas?"

"Actually," Fizz said, grinning mischievously, "I have." And with that, she drew back her hand and punched Dawn squarely on the nose.

Lifting Dawn from the floor, with her nose bleeding and instantly swelling up to the size of a balloon, Fizz began dragging her to the front of the queue.

"'Scuse me!" she bellowed, closely followed by the other Dawn and Kevin, who was hovering somewhat embarrassedly behind.

"Emergency! Make way! We've got a casualty here! Priority for the injured! Priority for the sick and needy!"

It took almost fifteen minutes for them to barge their way to the front of the queue. They pushed past several Ryataars along the way, one or two Glumphs, at least half a dozen little Dragonians, all of whom were wearing the most ridiculous woolly hats and scarves, and they even managed to upset a being somewhere near the front of the queue that looked astonishingly like a Rygona Blimpleberger.

Very carefully, they crept past a Brute standing at the very front of the line.

Brutes are absolutely terrifying creatures: enormous, spiky and leathery-looking, they carry the most enormous obliterators you have ever seen which are called – Obliterators.

However, the one thing not many beings in the Galaxy know about Brutes is that they are excellent visual deterrents. That is to say, their mere presence is enough to enforce security: no one looking at a Brute and his Obliterator weapon would ever want to pick a fight with one. But Brutes, you see, are only good as *visual* deterrents, because they are in fact nothing more than great big ugly cowards. It's in their genetic make-up: they despise violence, hate the idea of killing and wouldn't harm a Tik Tak. They don't even really like contact sports or loud music.

Having sidled past the Brute (and gasping at the size and ferocity of his appearance), Dawn, Dawn, Fizz and Kevin reached the Customer Service desk.

Fizz was so astounded to see the clerk at the desk that she dropped Dawn like a hot potato, right on her broken nose. Dawn bellowed in pain as Fizz peered over the desk at the funny, red little being and said:

"You!?"

Squig looked up from the little pod behind the desk he was squeezed into, and his face immediately changed to a deep purple colour.

"You!?" he said. "I don't believe it!"

"I thought you worked in the Time Tunnels," Fizz said.

"That's my day job," Squig replied. "I do part-time here when I'm needed. Not that it's any of your business. Now ... can I help you?"

Nobody said anything.

"Um ..." Fizz began, but couldn't finish.

"Another mission from Queeg, is it?" Squig sneered, with a grin.

"Kind of ... I s'pose," Fizz replied. "I'm not actually sure what we're supposed to do."

There were groans all around them. As Dawn got to her feet, still clutching her bloody, throbbing nose, she got the distinct feeling that they were about to get in a lot of trouble from at least one, and possibly all, of the beings they had just pushed past to reach the front of the queue.

"Where do you want to go?" Squig asked, irritably.

"Where do we want to go?" Fizz repeated.

"Yes. Where do you want to go? Any planet, any time, any dimension – anywhere in the Galaxy," Squig snapped impatiently. "Where do you want to go?"

Fizz and Dawn exchanged puzzled glances.

"Do you mean to tell me that we can go anywhere in the Galaxy, to any point in time from here?"

"Come on, will ya?" a voice boomed from the back of the queue. Fizz spun round to see a rather unpleasant-looking Zirtovian with, as far as she could count, twelve heads glaring at her. The rest of the queue began shouting and screaming their frustration along with the Zirtovian.

"Hang on a minute!" Fizz screamed back, silencing the room. "We're trying to save the Galaxy ... do you mind?"

She turned back to Squig and leant over the desk, so her face was almost inside his squashed little pod with him.

"We can go anywhere, right?"

"Correct."

"Any time we want, right?"

"Again, your genius astounds me," Squig said, sarcastically. "Now – where is it you want to go?"

Dawn and Fizz smiled to each other.

"Trygonian Council Recovery Vessel, orbiting Earth. Friday, 12:25am, September 17th, 2005."

"Very specific, I must say," Squig replied, as he began stamping some official-looking papers and pushing a lot of mysterious-looking buttons.

"Feel like saving the entire Galaxy, mate?" Fizz said, smiling at Dawn. "Sorry about the nose, by the way."

"I deserved it, for what I said on Grakonia," Dawn replied, smiling herself. "And yes, I feel like saving the Galaxy. Shall we?"

The two girls and Kevin turned back to Squig who, for a change, was smiling, probably happy to be getting rid of them.

"I don't," a familiar voice said behind them

Dawn, Fizz and Kevin turned to see the other Dawn Gray standing perfectly still, glaring at them with cold, emotionless eyes. In her hand was what looked remarkably like a Brute's Obliterator; the Brute himself was looking down at the holster around his waist and wondering where his gun had gone. He looked at the little Earth girl who was holding his Obliterator and the penny seemed to drop. He ran, crying like a little baby and hid in a corner, trembling and shaking.

"I don't feel like saving the Galaxy today," the other Dawn Gray went on, softly. "Today … I feel like changing my life. Today I feel like being a lucky Dawn Gray for a change."

The other Dawn Gray, the unlucky, alternative Dawn Gray, trailed the Obliterator from Fizz and then to Dawn.

"Today …" she said menacingly, looking directly at Dawn, "I feel like having *your* life for a change."

36

species defined

Above Mantor the Grakonian sky swirled with misty reds and purples. The cursor blinked on Mantor's blank screen, awaiting a response, awaiting Species Definition.

Something was happening in the Galaxy high above Mantor; the swirling cloud was spinning faster and faster and flashes of lightning blindingly lit up the darkness.

And then it appeared. A Time Tunnel.

It shot down from space as a single flash of the blinding lightning came and went and, in that millisecond, the open end of the tunnel lay before Mantor, half submerged in the boggy undergrowth of Grakonia.

Mantor did not move – even when the strange, obviously badly-injured creature emerged from the tunnel.

The being was dressed in a kind of robe, but it was ripped and torn and seemed to be full of burn marks and black, smoky holes. It gasped and coughed for air, holding its head as it stumbled forward and collapsed on its knees at Mantor's feet.

Jevkaa Creebo looked up and Mantor recognised him at once. He also knew, at that very same moment, that Jevkaa was about to die.

Jevkaa's Liquisage was shattered on one side and the fluid, gel-like substance behind the clear mask was leaking and dripping down onto his robe. The remaining fluid behind his Liquisage was spinning and bubbling furiously, with different expressions appearing and then disappearing: expressions of pain and confusion.

"Mantor," Jevkaa gasped. "I know what you are."

Mantor reached down a clawed hand and placed it firmly under Jevkaa's chin, holding his head up to face him.

SPECIFY SPECIES DEFINITION

the message flashed up on Mantor's screen.

Jevkaa could hardly breathe, but still he managed a chuckle to himself as more of the fluid that was his very life source leaked through his shattered Liquisage.

"The Galaxy is destroying itself, Mantor," he whispered. "Look around you. That swirling mass of red cloud is the Eye of the Galaxy. It is no more. The very centre of the Galaxy, the nerve centre, the heart of the Space-Time Vortex is gone!"

SPECIFY SPECIES DEFINITION

"Your mother with it," Jevkaa added with his dying gasps, ignoring Mantor's instruction. "Your mother! Your creator! She is gone … gone with the Eye of the Galaxy. Soon there will be nothing left. You will be able to define your new species in any way you like! Do you understand? Everything will die! Only you will be left!"

Mantor's grip around Jevkaa's throat tightened as he ran the message again –

SPECIFY SPECIES DEFINITION

"I saw you ..." Jevkaa gasped. "From the Eye of the Galaxy ... saw what you became ... I understand ..."

SPECIFY SPECIES DEFINITION

Jevkaa collapsed on the ground and Mantor let him fall.

"You know what you have become," Jevkaa said. "I will not tell you. I have lost everything. Soon, no being will have anything either, not even a life to call their own. You have organic components, Mantor. You have an ability to define yourself, to choose what you want to be." Jevkaa reached a hand up to Mantor in a gesture of friendship and goodwill.

Mantor did not move.

Jevkaa's Liquisage was leaking badly now, the cracks in his mask opening wider. He could not lift his head off the ground; there was not enough fluid in his mask to form even a part of any expression.

"You think about it, Mantor," he whispered. "If you are soon to survive in whatever may be left of the Galaxy, if anything does remain ... alone, then you must learn to think ... to make choices ... to define yourself. You know ,.. you understand; I know you do and you know what you can do, you know what you have become. *You* define your species, Mantor. I beg of you, though ..."

Jevkaa held out his hand again in another peaceful gesture –

"... I served your mother and creator for many years, oversaw your creation, and I too think of you as a son.

Please, I beg of you … make the right definition, and make the right choices. You do have a choice, Mantor! If you can understand what you have become … then you can make a choice as to the path you follow."

Jevkaa reached his hand further out to the monstrous creation that he had, for so long now, looked upon as a huge part of his own life with Empress Garcea. He could not smile, he could not show any kind of facial expression; but inside himself he was smiling and hoping that Mantor would understand now, and choose correctly.

"Can you understand?" Jevkaa whispered with his last gasps. "Will you take my hand and show me that the path you are about to choose is the right path, the just path?"

Jevkaa did not say any more.

Mantor *had* understood; he *had* chosen. He formed a ball of destructive, red laser fire in his hand and unleashed it directly at the dying being lying on the ground before him, killing him instantly.

37

back to the beginning

"What the heck are you doing?!" Fizz screamed. As far as she was concerned, Dawn Gray had always been a complete and total pain in the bum. But *this* Dawn Gray, this ... *alternative*, unlucky Dawn Gray was just plain insane and, not to put too fine a point on it, a bigger pain in the bum.

The other Dawn Gray aimed the Obliterator at Fizz, Dawn and Kevin, and though her hand was shaking and she didn't exactly look much like a cold-blooded killer, she certainly sounded crazy enough to do something stupid.

Everyone else in the dull waiting room inside the TimeEgg had fled for cover (not that there was any: they mainly huddled in corners, as far away as possible from the direction the gun was pointing in). Only the four of them were left standing: Dawn, Fizz and Kevin facing the alternative Dawn Gray and all her crazy, insane ideas about changing history and time.

"You heard me!" the other Dawn Gray shouted, glaring at Dawn. "I want your life. Swapsies, huh? You take mine, see how you like it."

"Dawn ... listen," she took a step back away from her now seemingly-maniacal and psychotic namesake.

"I thought we could get through this together? I thought ... I mean, we said back on the planet that we could start afresh together, a whole new life together ..."

"You said that?" Fizz suddenly exclaimed, looking at Dawn in complete amazement. "You're as bonkers as she is! Mind you, I don't know why I'm surprised. Two Dawn Grays, two people the same ... two people just as mental as each other."

"We are not the SAME!" the other Dawn Gray screeched. "How dare you even think that? Look at her ... in her posh, expensive pink pyjamas and stupid fluffy slippers . Who does she think she is? *We ll get through this together, Dawn ... start afresh together, Dawn ...* yeah, right! From the second that weird little freako roboboy turned up at Spectalica-Galactica, you've barely even looked my way, let alone asked me how I'm doing. Get through this together ... HA!"

"Why don't you just ... put the big, fat Obliterator down, huh, Dawn?" Fizz said, edging forward. "We don't really need a big, planet-destroying gun like that waving around now, do we? Hmm? We can just ... talk about this, can't we?"

"NO!"

The other Dawn Gray raised the Obliterator at Fizz, who stopped dead in her tracks. Kevin's shutters were down tight over his eyes and he hovered, inconspicuously low, above the counter Squig was still sitting behind, waiting for confirmation of everyone's travel details.

"I don't mean to interrupt," Squig said politely. "But there are people waiting. Are you going to agree on a destination this century or shall I put you on hold?"

"I told you!" Fizz bellowed. "Trygonian Council Recovery Vessel, orbiting Earth. Friday, 12:25am September 17th, 2005."

"No," the other Dawn Gray interrupted. "Earth, Queen Mary's Hospital, maternity ward, July 30th, 1992."

Fizz's face was blank as she turned to Dawn.

"My birthday," Dawn said.

"*Our* birthday," the other Dawn corrected her. "Your time, your dimension, your family, your life. Only difference being … you're not going back into it. I am."

"What's the point of that?" Fizz said, bluntly. "The Galaxy's destroying itself; time's ending. You'll still have your mum's umbilical cord attached to you when the Earth implodes to the size of a speck of dust!"

"I don't care!"

"You don't care? Oh, that's a good comeback. I want your life, I want this, I want that: I don't care if I die before I can even open my eyes."

"I want to be the other Dawn Gray for a change!"

"I want, I want, I want!" Fizz snapped. "Yeah, yeah, we heard ya."

"You don't know what it's like!"

The other Dawn Gray was getting upset, the Obliterator waving around in her hand dangerously erratically now, with Dawn and Kevin ducking every time the gun waved in their direction.

"Every other version of me, in every other time and dimension, had all the luck, all the breaks, all the money and good parents and good background – and what do I get? Orphaned … penniless, bullied, ugly, unlucky and DOOMED! YOU DON'T KNOW WHAT THAT'S LIKE! I want to be her! I want to be the Dawn Gray in expensive pink pyjamas and fluffy slippers, with a life and a family to go back to. I want to be HER!!!"

"If you don't let us go back and save the Earth and the rest of the Galaxy," Fizz screamed, "there'll be nothing to go back to, you big, crazy weirdo!"

The other Dawn Gray turned to Squig again.

"Earth, Queen Mary's Hospital, maternity ward, July 30th, 1992. Tickets or whatever I need, now, please."

"We don't do tickets, " Squig replied, calmly. "Simply an exit portal. The destination's programmed in … the destination is waiting the other side."

"Don't do it," Fizz said to Squig. "Please, the destination I gave you, or you won't live long enough to enjoy another rivetting shift in the Time Tunnel."

"Oh, and I'm supposed to believe that the Galaxy is coming to an end like you say it is, am I?" Squig smirked at Fizz. "That your mission – from the great Time Regulator Queeg, was it? He asked you to save the Galaxy, did he?"

"Yeah," Fizz replied, coldly. "He did. Trygonian Ship, please."

Squig studied Fizz for a moment, apparently trying to work out whether she was telling the truth or not. He knew Queeg well; had even worked for him on a few occasions. Queeg was a being Squig both admired and respected.

Fizz, however, he neither admired nor respected the slightest little bit.

"I can't transport two beings who are the same, from different dimensions in time, to the same point in the Galaxy," Squig said, almost apologetically. "One Dawn Gray can go; the other must stay."

"I'm going," the other Dawn Gray said. "Everyone else is staying here."

Squig looked at Fizz.

Fizz looked at Squig and then at Dawn.

Dawn looked at her other self.

Kevin … hid behind Squig's desk.

"Okay," Squig said. "I'll punch in the destination."

"Thank you," the other Dawn Gray said, smiling psychotically at Fizz and Dawn. "It's been fun," she said callously. "But I really have to be getting back to my new life now. See ya."

"Exit Portal 3B," Squig said, pointing to a white door that had just appeared out of nowhere.

The other Dawn Gray walked to the door, keeping her enormous gun trained on Fizz and Dawn. She waited – waited for her new life to begin, a life she had only dreamed of … a life she thought could never be hers.

"Ironic, isn't it?" Fizz whispered into Dawn's ear. "After everything we've been through, all the stuff we've overcome, we finally get beaten … finally lose out and condemn the Galaxy and everything in it to certain death … by you. Of all the people, of all the dangerous things and creatures in dimensions right across space and time … you sign your own death warrant, and mine, and everyone else's. Funny, really, ain't it?"

Dawn just glared at Fizz.

"Not really," she said.

Exit Portal 3B opened up with a *Zzzzziiip* and the other Dawn Gray was immediately faced with a humming, crackling, luminous blue grid.

"What the …?"

"The Space-Time Vortex!" Fizz and Dawn said in unison.

Suddenly the other Dawn Gray was sent flying back across the room, where she ended up on her back, the Obliterator flying from her hand.

Fizz raced across to get the gun and, standing up, looked across at the exit portal to find Dawn throwing her arms around someone in an embrace of love and joy.

It was Zak.

"Come on!" Zak cried out. "Your destination point is the other side of the Vortex. There isn't much time!"

He looked down at Dawn and smiled.

"See … I told you I'd look after you and help you do this, didn't I?"

Fizz looked across at Squig.

The little red creature was grinning at her.

"What can I say?" he said, shrugging his shoulders as best he could in his cramped little pod. "I believe you."

Fizz smiled as she handed the Obliterator back to the Brute who, along with everyone else, was getting back to his feet and trying to look as tough and calm as he had before he had run for cover from the little thirteen-year-old Earth girl.

Dawn and Zak walked through Exit Portal 3B and Fizz followed them. At the exit, she turned back to Squig.

"What about her?" she said, looking down at Dawn.

"She'll go back to where she belongs," Squig replied.

Fizz couldn't help but feel a twinge of pity for the alternative Dawn Gray. After all, all she had wanted to do was give herself a better a life – and why shouldn't she have, after the miserable luck and terrible existence she'd had?

"Those are the rules of space and time," Squig said, seeming to sense what Fizz was going to say next.

"Put her somewhere a bit nicer, eh?" Fizz said. "Back in her own time in space, sure, but give her an adopted family who'll love her and look after her, yeah?"

Squig smiled at Fizz and nodded.

"Thanks," Fizz said. "See ya round."

"I'm sure you will, Galaxy Guide," Squig replied, perhaps to himself.

And with that, Fizz hopped through the Exit Portal.

"Sowwy about all that," Kevin mumbled, as he flew along behind Fizz. "Weally was a tewwible mess, wasn't it? Earthlings ... I'll never understand them. Bye!"

And with that, he vanished through the Exit Portal, through the Vortex and ended up ...

... back aboard the Trygonian Council Recovery Vessel, with Fizz, Dawn and Zak standing right beside him.

Below them, through a small porthole window, the Earth, still there … still safe. But … for how much longer?

38

the shape-shifter

"We've got to get to the bridge!" Fizz screamed.

They had all appeared in the cargo hold of the ship, back where Dawn and Fizz had first met Kevin, back when they first DROSSed off the Earth – what now seemed like years ago.

"Jowlox!" Dawn cried.

"Me old mate," Fizz smiled.

"Jowlox?" Zak echoed. "Who's Jowlox?"

Dawn and Fizz shared a smile.

"Don't worry, it's a long story," Fizz chuckled. "Just follow me, and on the way to the bridge you can tell us just what the heck happened to you and how you ended up here."

Kevin led the way to the bridge; nobody remembered the Trygonian Ship better than he did. He had been a service droid for the ship and its crew of Likk-Lax for a good few aeons; he was thrilled to be back again and, in a bizarre way, was looking forward to seeing Jowlox once more.

"So who is this Jowlox?" Zak called, as he raced along the winding corridors behind Fizz and Dawn.

"He's a shape-shifter!" Fizz called back.

"A what?"

"A shape-shifter," Dawn repeated. "He's a being known as a Mimicaabus. He can replicate and form any shape of any other living being."

"Yeah. He even manages to form his own interpretations of emotions as well," Fizz added, remembering the horrible experience she had had with Jowlox when he tried to replicate the human expression known as a hug in order to persuade her to stay on the ship with him.

"So what's your story then, Stitch?" Fizz said. "Last time I saw you, you were being dragged into the swamp on Grakonia."

"Yeah, well … they didn't like the taste of me, I s'pose!" Zak called out, smiling at Dawn. Dawn reached behind her and took his hand as she ran.

"I'm glad they didn't like the taste of you," she said, softly. "Blimey, your hand is freezing, are you okay?"

"That'll be travelling though the Exit Portal," Fizz called back to the pair. "My hands are cold too. It's not like LX Travel or Time Tunnel travel. Walking through an Exit Portal is a bit like being frozen in time and being dumped back in the spot where you want to be."

Dawn squeezed Zak's hand more tightly.

"I'm just glad you're here," she said. "I thought I'd lost you."

"No way," Zak replied. " 'Soon as I saw that TimeEgg, once I was out of the swamp, I was through it. Ended up on the other side of the Exit Portal, though. I heard what was going on between you lot. When the door zipped up and I saw that other Dawn standing there, all I could think to do was to get that gun from her."

"Yeah …" Fizz said, more to herself than to Dawn and Zak. "Lucky you were there, huh? Right behind the exact Exit Portal she was coming out of … what a bit of luck, huh?"

Suddenly, they came to a huge door and everyone stopped.

"The bwidge," Kevin said, and almost as though the ship itself had been expecting them … the door sprang up, revealing the vast, dark, almost empty room beyond.

Jowlox the One was sitting where he had been the first time Dawn and Fizz had been here with Kevin. Across the huge room, through the darkness, in a giant, leather swivel chair, sat a little girl with pigtails and pretty little sandals on her feet.

"Uh…" whispered Zak, confused. "That's a little Earth girl, isn't it?"

"That's Jowlox," Dawn replied, still holding Zak's hand. "He hijacked this ship from the Likk-Lax, who were driving it for the Trygonian Council to relocate the Earth. He stowed away here, knowing that when the Earth was towed he could just transport himself down onto the planet's surface. He thought that if he looked like an Earth child, he would fit in and no questions would be asked."

"That was his plan?" Zak said, disbelievingly.

"That's just part of it, but there isn't time for that now," Fizz said, looking out of a nearby porthole window.

"Clock's ticking, and we're right over the Earth. It must be nearly time to tow it – we've gotta get going."

"Going with what?" Dawn said, suddenly realising that she didn't have the faintest idea what they were going to do to stop the Earth from being towed and relocated. "What are we supposed to do?"

Fizz pulled the last TimeEgg out of her bag and held it up.

"I … don't know," she said.

"What?!" Dawn screamed. "You don't know? What do you mean, you don't know? The Earth is about be relocated again, Fizz, and we've been asked to stop it! How can you not know?"

"Look," Fizz said, defensively. "Queeg told me to use the TimeEgg in the way that you and I saw best to do the job. So if you've got any ideas, now's the time to let me have them."

Dawn let go of Zak's freezing cold hand and walked across the bridge to Jowlox.

"We ask Jowlox," she said, spinning the leather chair around to face the little girl. "You know what happens aboard this ship to release the tow cable, don't you, Jowlox?"

Jowlox was slumped in the chair. The little girl's head flopped down on her chest. "What's the matter with him?" Dawn said.

"I don't know," said Fizz, scrambling over to Jowlox to get a better look at him.

"Look!" Zak called out, and Dawn and Fizz looked up at a control panel on the ship's main computer that read:

TOW CABLE BEING RELEASED.

ATTACHMENT TO EARTH
IN T MINUS 2 MINUTES.

"Okay …" Fizz said, panic-stricken. "We've got two minutes. Two minutes! Think Dawn. Think Kevin. Think Zak!"

The Earth grew larger in the porthole window as it got closer to the ship, whilst Dawn, Fizz, Kevin and Zak scrambled around the bridge of the ship trying to find something … some way … to stop the towing process, which was clearly pre-programmed and couldn't be overridden or stopped.

There had to be something … something they could use the TimeEgg on, something they could freeze and stop in time that would prevent the Earth's destruction, and subsequently the destruction of the Galaxy.

"This is hopeless!" Dawn cried out desperately. "This big hunk-of-rubbish spaceship is going to destroy my home again!"

Suddenly Fizz screamed.

"That's it! I've got it!" Fizz, Zak and Kevin spun round and saw Fizz gazing out of the huge viewing window at the enormous Earth that was getting ever closer to the ship.

"Rubbish!" Fizz exclaimed.

"Eh?" Dawn said, reaching out for Zak's hand and finding it colder than ever.

"This ship, like any other space vessel, especially commercial vessels, has rubbish-disposal chutes, two of them. We crack the egg open," Fizz went on explaining, "and fire the two halves out into space. The two halves will separate; one will float through space one side of the Earth, the other on the other side. Everything between the two halves, including planet Earth itself, will be frozen in time and perfectly safe."

There was silence as everyone considered Fizz's lunatic plan.

"You know something …" Dawn finally said. "That's actually quite a good idea."

"I know!" Fizz screamed.

Kevin led the way down to the rubbish-disposal level – Level 90 – the last level on the ship. Dawn, Fizz and Zak followed the little robot as he led them to two enormous funnels sticking out of the wall.

"Are we facing the Earth?" Dawn said.

"Our angle and twajectowy are cowwect," Kevin said. "As long as twavelling down the chutes doesn't actually shatter the TimeEgg shells, they'll fly out of the fwont of the ship and pwopel themselves towards the Earth."

"Nice one, Kev," Fizz said. "Let's just hope this works."

She lifted the egg to crack the shell before a strange, mixed voice, unfamiliar to everyone, said:

"Stop!"

Fizz turned round and found herself face to face with Zak, only … it wasn't quite Zak. It was something horrible, something terrifying something … well, quite frankly, nobody had ever seen anything like it before. It was like a whole new species.

"What the …?" Fizz gasped.

"Zak?!" Dawn screamed.

Kevin snapped the shutters down over his eyes again and waited, hoping somebody would find a way for them to get out of this one.

Zak suddenly appeared to Fizz and Dawn to be made of some kind of … well … jelly I suppose. He wobbled and his body rippled, as it seemed to mould and resculpt itself in much the same way as …

"You're a shape-shifter?" Fizz said.

Zak just chuckled, his laugh deepening as it changed tone and texture. The image of his face and head melted away, as did the shape of his body, and he became not much more than a big gelatinous blob of rubbery-looking … stuff.

Dawn and Fizz recoiled in surprise and horror as the thing that had been Zak grew upwards and outwards.

The thing threw its head back and screamed as it stretched and widened, and its frame and skin seemed to harden.

"I … AM … NOT … A … SHAPE-SHIFTER!" the thing screamed, before finally it stopped and Dawn and Fizz found themselves standing open-mouthed in horror and terror.

The thing before them twitched slightly as it settled back into what Dawn and Fizz assumed was its natural form.

It lifted its head.

The black screen embedded in the front of the creature's skull flickered.

A message ran across it:

I AM MANTOR

it read.

Fizz remembered Jowlox motionless, lifeless, in his chair and it all suddenly became clear.

Jowlox was dead.

Now … *he* was Mantor.

Now Dawn, Fizz and Kevin were trapped again.

And this time, there really was no way out.

"Nice knowing you, Dawn Gray," Fizz whispered.

"Giving up already?" Dawn replied softly, backing herself against the wall, as far away from Mantor as she could get. "I expected better from you."

The ball of burning red laser fire began growing and hissing in Mantor's hand again.

SPACE-TIME MANIPULATOR
MUST BE TERMINATED.

the message on Mantor's screen read.

MUST BE TERMINATED … NOW

"You can expect all you like, mate," Fizz said, putting a hand out and holding onto Kevin. "I'm fresh out of suggestions. You got any brilliant ideas?"

"Not yet," Dawn replied. "But there's still time."

"I hate to tell you this, Dawn," Fizz said. "But our time is well and truly up."

Dawn just smiled.

"Trust me," she said. "There's still time."

epilogue

Far below the Trygonian Council Recovery Vessel, where Dawn, Fizz and Kevin were facing their fate at the hands of a reborn Mantor, the people of Earth, the residents of Kirkland Street, were running around screaming in terror as they watched the enormous spaceship descend from the dark, starry sky.

The electric-blue tow cable had been released from the Trygonian ship and was in the process of attaching itself to the Earth.

There were now only seconds before the Earth was towed away and all life on the planet would be doomed.

Amongst the screaming, panicking residents of Kirkland Street, two people, two young girls, stared up at the Trygonian ship in curiosity.

"It's early," the first girl said.

"You reckon?" the other girl replied checking her watch. "I'd say it was about bang on time."

The two girls looked at each other and smiled. Around them panic-stricken screams filled the air, but the girls knew the chain of events off by heart by now.

"You ready to do this?" the first girl said, looking back up at the Trygonian ship.

"I don't know what *this* is yet," the other girl replied. "And anyway, the question is, are you sure? I mean, you're still in your pyjamas; don't you ever change?"

Dawn looked at Fizz and smiled again.

"Like I get the time to change!" she said. "With you around, there's never time to do anything except run around and save planets and Galaxies, and risk my life with one intergalactic menace after another."

Fizz threw her arm around her friend's shoulder and together they looked out across the lawn at Dawn's parents, who were sitting safe and sound in the centre of their front garden.

"They've been frozen all this time?" Dawn said.

"Ever since Queeg came down and saw me, yeah," Fizz replied. "I wonder what happened to him?"

"I'd like to know," Dawn replied. "I wanna thank him for saving my parents' lives. Anyway, we've got no time left. Ready?"

"Ready for what?" Fizz replied. "For once, Dawn Gray, you've lost me. What exactly is it that you want to do?"

Dawn grinned to herself as she pulled a swimming hat over her head, donned a pair of sunglasses and earmuffs and began applying sunblock all over her face.

Slowly, the Earth began to rock slightly. It was like the beginning of an earthquake erupting beneath the ground.

Everyone began screaming louder than before, as the Earth slowly began to tilt.

It was being towed.

It was being relocated.

This was it … the Earth was finished.

"Just get ready, will ya?" Dawn said. "I've just had this brilliant idea."